A chill, a silent warning, touched
the edge of Ki's mind...

Instinctively, his body dropped into a fighting crouch,
legs bent slightly at the knees, hands held away from
his sides. He could see nothing at all in the dense gray
world around him, hear nothing but the silence.

He moved a step forward and then stopped, going
nearly to the ground. Ahead, four men suddenly appeared before his eyes. They were there for an instant,
then gone, wraiths swallowed up in the fog. Still, they
were visible long enough—Ki saw all he needed to
see.

He followed, keeping to the cover of the fog. A building loomed up before him. Once more, the cold presence of his enemy reached out to touch him. As he
raced for the door that now stood open to the fog, a
high-pitched scream reached his ears...

◆■◆ WESLEY ELLIS ◆■◆

LONE STAR

AND THE ALASKAN GUNS

A JOVE BOOK

LONE STAR AND THE ALASKAN GUNS

A Jove Book/published by arrangement with
the author

PRINTING HISTORY
Jove edition/December 1985

ISBN: 0-515-08423-9

Jove books are published by The Berkley Publishing Group,
200 Madison Avenue, New York, N.Y. 10016. The words
"A JOVE BOOK" and the "J" with sunburst are trademarks
belonging to Jove Publications, Inc.

PRINTED IN THE UNITED STATES OF AMERICA

Chapter 1

"We'll be putting ashore up ahead," said Captain Griffin, "right over there past Customs House." Leaning over the steamer's brass railing, he squinted into the wind across the slate-blue water. "See there?" he pointed. "That's St. Michael's. And up on the hill's old Baranov's castle—the Roosian feller that settled this place after he kicked out the Injuns."

"It's lovely," said Jessica Starbuck, "it really is."

It was a long way back, Jessie reflected. A thousand miles on the once-a-month steamer from Portland, up past Vancouver Island and the shores of British Columbia. And this long strip of islands sheltering Sitka was only the tail end of Alaska. The real bulk of that enormous land didn't begin for another three hundred miles. It was hard even to imagine such a place— twice the size of Texas—and men had scarcely begun to chart its vast stretches of wilderness.

Jessie turned as Ki rounded a corner of the deck, clutching their valises in both hands and under his arms. She shook her head as he eased the whole load onto the wooden planking.

1

"I would have helped you with that if you'd asked," she said. "You didn't have to do it all."

"I think I got everything," he told her. Straightening, he ran a hand through his raven-black hair. "I've seen cooler days than this in San Antone," he muttered. "I thought we were coming to the great frozen north."

"Not that frozen—and not *that* far north, either," she reminded him. "And this is summer, Ki. A few months from now it won't be this pleasant."

"A few months from now, we'd better be back in Texas," he said flatly.

Jessie laughed and looked past him at the docks looming close beyond the starboard prow of the ship. The steamer's arrival was a big event in Sitka, and over a hundred people were on hand to witness the landing. Jessie searched among the faces, looking for a man who might be Hiram Platte, her manager for the Starbuck interests in Alaska. It was Platte's alarming letter that had started her on the long journey north from the Circle Star Ranch. Several cargo vessels had been lost under suspicious circumstances. Warehouses and stores had burned to the ground in Sitka and at Wrangell to the south. A number of merchants had been forced out of business, frightened into selling at a loss. Two of the ships and one of the warehouses had belonged to Jessie.

Platte's message spoke of the increasing presence of a business adventurer known as Kodiak Burke. The name had alerted Jessie at once. Harold Edmund Burke was the subject of a highly secret document that had come to her attention the year before, a document naming several men involved in the Prussian business cartel's affairs in the Canadian northwest. If Burke were now operating in Alaska, Jessie was certain the cartel had taken a keen interest in the United States's newest possession.

The steamer's big engines shuddered to a stop; seamen secured their lines and raised the sloping gangway from the dock.

"You see anyone who looks like he knows us?" Ki picked up his load of valises again.

"No one," Jessie told him, "but that doesn't mean a thing. I wouldn't know Platte if I saw him. Come on, now, give me

2

a couple of those bags. I'm not crippled, Ki."

Leaving the steamer, Jessie studied the people below once more. As her gaze swept the crowd, a single face caught her eyes and held them. It wasn't hard to pick him out—he was six feet three or more if he was an inch, a head taller than most of the bearded, hollow-eyed miners and the stocky, broad-shouldered Indians who'd gathered to watch. His eyes were black as river stones, set above a prominent, hawklike nose. His face appeared hard, roughly chiseled out of stone. When he smiled, though, catching Jessie's eye, his features softened in a manner she found most appealing. *I don't know who you are, mister, but I wouldn't mind saying hello.* She returned his smile and looked away, searching once more for Hiram Platte. When she glanced back to find the stranger again, he was gone.

"He's got to know we're here," Jessie said wryly. "It'd be kinda hard to sneak into Sitka unnoticed." She set down her coffee and shook her head. "Ki, this place is *dead*, you know? Did you see the buildings and houses as we came through town? Half of them are empty—boarded up or just abandoned!"

"It isn't real lively," Ki agreed. He bit his lip and frowned in thought. "Maybe this Platte never got your letter."

"Uh-huh. I thought of that, but I don't think so. I paid a premium to make sure that message got on the first ship coming up here. It didn't wait for the steamer." She made a face and stared suspiciously at the bite of meat on her fork. "What do you suppose this is I'm eating—*moose,* maybe?"

Ki grinned. "I already asked. It's caribou."

"They must have chased this one all the way down from the Arctic Circle," Jessie grumbled. "I've tasted saddle leather easier to chew."

Earlier, they'd checked into the town's only hotel, a narrow, clapboard structure called The Grande Pacific. As far as Ki was concerned, the only thing grand about the place was its name. The closet-size rooms were damp and dirty, and the beds smelled of mildew and too many bodies. Ki had changed quickly and met Jessie next door at the equally unimposing Sitka Café.

Ki wiped a napkin across his face and pushed back his chair.

"Look, why don't you finish up your coffee? I'll take a quick walk and see if I can turn up Platte. Meet you back at the hotel."

"Go ahead," said Jessie. "From the looks of this place, you ought to be back in about three minutes."

Ki nodded, then stood and walked out the front door. Jessie watched until he crossed the narrow street and disappeared around a corner. The coffee wasn't all that good, but she ordered another cup. At least, it beat walking next door to the hotel and doing nothing. Her room had all the comfort and refinement of a cell.

Jessie glanced up as the café door opened. A young officer in navy blues stepped in, saw Jessie, and walked quickly to her table.

"Begging your pardon, ma'am," he said, "but you'd be Miss Jessica Starbuck, would you not?"

"I am," Jessie told him, "and you would be—?"

"Lieutenant Joshua Gray, miss. United States Navy." He whisked off his cap and gave her a foolish little bow. "Welcome to Sitka, Miss Starbuck. Captain Beardslee sends his compliments and hopes you'll find your stay here enjoyable. An impossible task, I might add—but he welcomes you nonetheless."

Jessie smiled politely. "Won't you join me for coffee, Lieutenant? And thank you for the welcome. And the warning as well."

Gray took Ki's chair, perching on the edge. For some reason, Jessie noted, he was nervous, uneasy at the invitation. He was a stocky young man with a ruddy complexion and had wavy, straw-colored hair and a sweeping handlebar mustache to match. Presentable enough, thought Jessie. Nearly handsome, except for the eyes. They were close set and a pale, almost watery blue. They seemed to dart about from one object to the other, unsure of where to settle.

"I would have met your steamer," Gray said quickly, "but, ah—other duties prevailed. There's not a *lot* to do up here, you understand, but the captain, he likes to keep his officers busy." He gave Jessie a sheepish grin. "That's the navy for you, I guess."

4

Jessie set down her cup and gave him a curious look. "Your commanding officer, Lieutenant, he—Captain Beardslee, is it?—he knew I was coming in today?"

"Well, yes ma'am, he did."

"I wonder how that could be. Only one man in Sitka knew I was coming, and I doubt that he'd share that confidence with anyone else."

"Ah, certainly. I understand." Gray shifted uncomfortably and looked at his hands. "That's really why I'm here, you see, miss. We found a letter saying you were coming. That's how we happened to know."

"You *found* a letter?" Jessie sat up straight. Gray's words had telegraphed a warning; she was afraid she knew what had to come next. "You found a letter where, Lieutenant?"

"It was among Mr. Hiram Platte's effects." Gray held her gaze a quick moment. "I'm afraid he's dead," he said, letting all the words spill out at once, "just as dead as he can be!"

"Yes, of course." Jessie briefly closed her eyes. "What happened exactly? How long has he been dead?"

"Nine days today. And it was murder, ma'am. Murder pure and simple."

"*Murder!*" Jessie stared. "Who killed him, do you know?"

A small tic began at the corner of Gray's mouth. Jessie noticed tiny beads of sweat on his brow. "It was one of the Tlinglts, the Injuns who live around the islands."

"I know who they are," said Jessie.

"Well, they're a sorry lot, I'll tell you." Gray's hands began to shake. "Carved up poor Mr. Platte with one of those bone-handled knives. Should have wiped out every one of the b—bastards a long time a—" Gray stopped and stared at Jessie like an owl. "Uh, excuse me, miss—I'll be right back—"

Before Jessie could answer, Gray jerked up and sent his chair rattling across the floor. She watched, puzzled, as he stumbled across the room and bolted into the street.

"Now what's all that about?" she muttered under her breath. Maybe the poor man had to relieve himself. If that were so, he had a really terrible problem.

Lord, it's starting already, she thought soberly. She didn't

5

believe Gray's story about Indians for a minute. Somehow, she was sure Kodiak Burke was involved. Maybe her careful, ever cautious manager had made a mistake. If Burke had learned Platte was interested in his Alaskan operations, he wouldn't have hesitated an instant to put an end to the man's curiosity. And if Burke didn't already know she was in Sitka, someone would tell him soon enough. Jessie wasn't fool enough to imagine he didn't know who she was. There was scarcely a man in the cartel's employ who didn't know her name, who wouldn't recognize her at once. That shadowy organization knew its enemies as well as its friends.

Jessie turned as Joshua Gray appeared in the café once more. Whatever his concern might have been, it seemed to have vanished abruptly. There was a new spring in his step, a lively glint in his eyes.

"Sorry," he grinned, dropping heavily into his chair. "Didn't mean to run off like that."

"Are you all right, Lieutenant?"

"Fine, just fine, miss. Now . . ." He spread his broad hands on the table. "You just tell me how I can help. Know Mr. Platte's tragic demise must've come as a shock. When you feel more like it, why, I'd be pleased to escort you to his office. Not real far from here."

"I feel fine right now," Jessie assured him, "and I do want to see that office. First, though, I'd like to know more about Mr. Platte's murder—where it happened, the circumstances. If you could direct me to the marshal's office or the local sheriff."

Gray threw back his head in a raucous laugh. Jessie looked startled, and he raised an apologetic hand. "Sorry. You don't know much about Sitka, now do you? There isn't any lawman—'cause there isn't any *law*. 'Less you count the U.S. Naval Regulations. Town Council folded last year, right before we sailed in on the *Jamestown*. Captain Lester A. Beardslee's all the *official* government you're going to find in Alaska."

"That's ridiculous," Jessie said stiffly.

"Of course it is. But it's true." He leaned in close and showed her a lopsided grin. Jessie backed off at once; she suddenly understood Gray's new burst of energy, the startling change in

6

his manner. His breath told the story and explained his abrupt departure. Lieutenant Gray was a drinker, most likely a dedicated drunk. Talking about Platte had made him nervous, and he'd left to renew his courage.

"Thank you for your time, Lieutenant," Jessie said coolly. She stood, reached into her purse, and scattered coins on the table. "And please thank Captain Beardslee for his kindness."

"Uh, you're not leaving, are you?" Gray blinked in surprise.

"Yes, Lieutenant, I am," Jessie said politely. She smiled and brushed past him, opened the door and stepped outside. Gray caught up with her at once, pasting a quick smile on his face.

"If you'd—uh—like to go over to Platte's office, I can show you the way now."

"No, thank you. I think I'd like to handle that later."

"Well, I'll just walk you back to the hotel, then."

Jessie stopped on the wooden sidewalk and looked him squarely in the eye. "Lieutenant Gray, you already have. You see, the hotel's right there."

"What d'you know 'bout that?" He showed her a foolish grin. "In that case, better see you to your room."

"I don't think so," Jessie said stiffly. "What you'd better do, friend, is go somewhere and sober up." She opened the door and stalked quickly past him. As she turned away, she caught the furtive eyes that swept past her breasts and moved to the curve of her hips. His look brought a hot flush of anger to her cheeks. For the most part, Jessie Starbuck welcomed a man's admiring glance. If the occasion were right, she might boldly return the look in kind. But an open, honest exchange was one thing—a glance like Joshua Gray's was something else.

Crossing the small lobby, she lifted her skirts and hurriedly climbed the narrow stairs to the second floor. She was angry at Gray and furious at herself. Why had she let him force her out of the café, back to her dismal room? Damn it all, anyway—one place to sit in town and she'd allowed some drunken fool to chase her off! She should have stood her ground, told him exactly what she—

Jessie froze, turned swiftly, and saw Gray lumbering toward

7

her down the hall. "Now look," she said coldly, "if you know what's good for you, Lieutenant, you'll turn right around and go back downstairs!"

"Hey, now, I already *know* what's good for me." He leered and showed his teeth. "You're the prettiest little thing I ever saw, Miss Starbuck. Honest to God you are!"

"Thanks a lot," Jessie said darkly, "now back off and—*damn it, Gray, no!*"

She raised her hand to stop him and he gripped her wrist hard, wrenching the room key from her and forcing her flat against the door. Jessie struggled against his bulk as he fumbled with the key, opened the door, and shoved her roughly inside. Jessie went sprawling, caught herself on the iron bedstead, and ran for the small window to her right. There was an overhanging roof; past that, the drop to the ground would be—

Gray caught the circle of her waist, lifted her off the floor, and turned her around to face him. His hand found the bodice of her dress and ripped the fabric away. Jessie pounded his chest and raked her hands across his face. Gray cried out in anger, seized her wrists, and slapped her hard. Jessie gasped, tears of pain blurring her eyes. Gray pulled her to him and tore at the shreds of her dress, then jerked the thin chemise off her shoulders.

"Good G–God Almighty!" Gray stared in open wonder as the taut, creamy globes of flesh sprang free. Jessie covered herself with her hands and backed away. Gray reached a trembling hand under his jacket and brought out a silver flask. He took a long swallow and set the flask aside.

"You're going to get it," he said hoarsely, wiping one sleeve across his mouth. "You can f–fight me or make it easy. Up to you, lady."

Jessie took a calming breath. "Look, just don't hurt me, all right?" She backed up slowly and perched on the edge of the bed. "See, I'm going to give you what you want, okay?"

"Yeah, yeah, okay." Gray stood woodenly, his legs swaying slightly. He reached for the flask again. "Just hurry it up, you hear?"

"Not *too* fast, though." Jessie forced an impish grin. "Too

8

fast spoils all the fun." She raised her skirts slowly, baring the long, silken lines of her legs. "How's that look to you, huh?"

"Jesus . . ." Gray moaned.

Jessie slid the skirts past her knees to the sleek flanks of her thighs. Gray's mouth fell open. His eyes darted from her breasts to the lovely expanse of flesh down below. Jessie's left hand moved in a slow, lazy circle between her legs. Her right hand moved in a blur—the ivory-handled derringer slipped free of its garter holster; the twin barrels steadied on a spot between Joshua Gray's eyes.

"Huh?" Gray blinked in sudden horror. "Hey, now wait!"

"Mister, your lovin' days are over," Jessie said tightly. Her green eyes smoldered. "If you ever had any, and I've got my doubts about that."

"Look, I—" Gray's face drained of color. "I never meant anything. I made a mistake."

"You sure as hell did." Jessie lowered the pistol until it pointed directly between his legs. "One . . . two . . ."

"My God, *no!*" Gray shrieked.

"Three!"

Gray's features went slack. His eyes rolled back in his head and the breath left his mouth in a whisper. His legs suddenly collapsed and he fell to the floor like a sack.

Jessie stood and thrust her hands on her hips in disgust. "Great. Now what am I supposed to do with you?" She pulled the tattered remains of her dress about her breasts and started rolling Joshua Gray toward the door with her foot. "Welcome to Alaska, Jessie Starbuck," she muttered under her breath. "You're going to love it up here."

Chapter 2

Leaden clouds pressed the earth, turning the day a somber shade of gray. The inland mountains had vanished, lost in a curtain of mist. Ki followed the wooden sidewalks, making his way east from the Sitka Café. The drab buildings, packed closely together, scarcely had room for an alley between their peeling clapboard walls.

Turning into Lincoln Street, he came upon the flat, narrow expanse of the Sitka Trading Company. The building was nearly sixty yards long, the only structure he'd seen that didn't need paint. Ki hesitated an instant, then turned and walked north. The trading company was clearly one of the town's gathering places—a good place to pick up information, a bad one to start asking questions. He needed to find Platte, but he also wanted to learn what he could about Kodiak Burke. Burke would know who they were soon enough—Ki saw no reason to hang out a sign.

A block up the street, Ki looked to his left and found what he wanted. The store was built of sturdy yellow cedar. The neatly painted sign above the door read:

Ki decided there wouldn't be many customers inside. With luck, he'd get answers to his questions without attracting undue attention.

Inside, Ki walked the length of the place and back, picked up a nasty looking wolf trap and returned it gingerly to the counter. Whoever was running the place clearly wasn't eager for customers. Maybe, he decided, there simply weren't enough customers in Sitka to go around. With the big trading company down the street—

"Yes? Can I help you find something?"

Ki turned, surprised to find he wasn't alone. The girl stepped from behind the counter as if she'd been there all along. Ki stared, drew in a breath, and held it. "Uh, no. Thank you," he said quickly. "I was just looking."

"Yes, I see you were." A flicker of amusement touched the corners of her mouth, vanishing almost at once.

"I'm new in town," Ki told her. "I saw your store and just walked in. You've sure got some interesting goods in here." He knew at once the words sounded foolish. He picked up the wolf trap again and studied it with great interest.

"Are you thinking about doing some trapping?" the girl said coolly

"No." Ki set the trap down at once. "Just never saw one quite like it before." He knew he was still staring and couldn't help it. He'd seldom felt ill at ease in the presence of a pretty girl. This one, though, was doing peculiar things to his head—and certain other parts of his body as well. She was tall for a woman, not too far from an even six feet. Her plain gingham dress clung to a lean, rangy figure. The dress failed to hide an incredibly slim waist, long, coltish legs, and pert little breasts as hard as apples. Even if he hadn't seen the sign above the door, her features would have given her away. The high, prominent bones of her cheeks, the wide cut of her mouth, betrayed her Slavic heritage. Her skin was pale cream kissed with olive; her hair was black and braided, caught in tight coils on either side of her head.

11

It was the eyes, though, that turned her from a fetching, attractive girl to a rare and striking beauty. Her eyes were enormous, glacier-blue in color and shaded by a thick veil of lashes that gave her a wanton, sleepy look. Ki had a sudden vision of this girl waking up in the morning—yawning, stretching long limbs, letting the lazy eyes touch his own . . .

"Ah, what?" Ki blinked and cleared his throat. "I'm sorry, you said something?"

"I *said*, if you don't want traps, is there something else you'd like to see?"

"There, one of those." Ki pointed quickly to the first thing he saw. "I'll take one of those, please."

"An axe handle."

"Right."

"What a careless man," she said solemnly. She lifted the shaft of wood from a rack and laid it on the counter. "Off the steamer from Portland only a few hours, and already you have broken an axe." She caught Ki's startled expression and burst into sudden laughter. "You don't want an axe handle," she scolded gently, "or anything else for that matter. Please. You are in here for something. Why don't you tell me what it is?"

Ki felt the color rise to his face. "I don't guess much happens in Sitka without everybody knowing."

"No. Not much. It is a very small town." She smiled and brushed a hand across her cheek. "My name is Natalia. Natalia Shelikhov. And you, you are traveling with the very pretty lady, and you are both staying at the hotel."

Ki showed her a sheepish grin. "I'd hate to try to keep a secret in this place."

"Oh, there are a great many secrets here," she said evenly. "Most of us know them all, of course, but we don't *tell* anyone that we do."

Ki smiled. "I am called Ki. And you're right, I don't have much use for an axe handle."

"Ki." She tasted the name on her lips. "And what is it you want to know, Ki? That *is* what you came for, isn't it? To ask questions?"

Ki nodded, looked at his hands, and faced her again. "I'm

trying to find someone. He was supposed to meet us here but he didn't show up."

"And his name?"

"His name's Hiram Platte and he's a—what is it, what's wrong?" He saw her eyes go wide, the color fade from her cheeks.

"Of course," she said under her breath, "the lady's name is Starbuck, yes? I should have put the two together."

"Put *what* together?"

"I'm sorry." She bit her lip and looked up from under her lashes. "Ki, Mr. Platte is dead. He was killed, I'm afraid."

"What?" Ki stared. "But how did it happen, when?"

"Enough, Natalia, you have told the gentleman all you know!"

Ki turned quickly to see a man step out of the dark doorway behind the counter. He was tall, thick-chested, a handsome man in his mid-fifties with a heavy black beard and eyes the same startling shade of blue as the girl's.

"Uncle," Natalia said hastily, "he's a friend, I'm sure. He is with the woman who—"

"Thank you, Natalia," the man said sharply, "I will decide for myself who is friend and who is not, *da?*" He glanced narrowly at Ki. "I am Nikolai Shelikhov. I sell things—everything you see here is for sale. You want to buy, fine. You want to talk, go to saloon or down to wharves. You find plenty people talk to you there."

"Uncle Nikolai!"

"Enough, Natalia!" His eyes sent the girl a harsh warning. "You don't hear me well? I have to say again?"

"Mr. Shelikhov," Ki said softly, "I didn't mean any harm asking questions. It isn't as if Mr. Platte's death is none of my business. It is. He worked for Jessie Starbuck. So do I. She has a right to know what happened to him."

"Hmmmph." The man gave Ki a grudging nod. "Maybe this is true. Who can say? Still, there is nothing more to tell. He is dead. You tell the lady that."

"No," Ki said, "that won't do it. Natalia here said he was killed. Who killed him?"

"A Kolosh, an Indian from the waterfront slums."

13

"Uncle, that's not true and you know it," Natalia said curtly.

"Girl, shut your mouth!" Shelikhov bellowed. His eyes blazed with anger, and for a moment Ki was certain he meant to strike her.

"No, I won't!" Natalia stood her ground. Her fists were planted firmly on her hips; her shapely jaw stuck out in fierce determination. "The whole town knows that's a lie, uncle. Mr. Platte was a good man—you shame him and yourself by telling such a story. The truth is the truth, and you can't change it by looking the other way!"

For an instant, pain replaced anger in the old man's eyes. "Go now; leave my store," he told Ki. "There is nothing here for you." He turned, then, passing Natalia without meeting her glance, and stalked angrily through the door behind the counter.

"Hell, I'm sorry," said Ki, "I didn't mean to start up any trouble."

"You couldn't possibly add more than there is," the girl said grimly. "Come on, I'll walk a ways with you. I've got to get out of here for a while."

Outside, a slight, misting rain had begun to fall, softening the harsh outlines of the town. Natalia closed her eyes and breathed the damp air with clear delight.

"People think we are crazy to live in Sitka," she said. "In the summer it rains all the time, and in the winter it is too cold to imagine. I love it—I wouldn't live anywhere else." She looked at Ki and laughed at her words. "That's a silly thing to say. I have never even been anywhere else!"

"And your uncle," Ki asked, "how long has he been here?"

"What? Oh, I see. You mean the accent, don't you? He's been here all his life, Ki. He was born here. You must understand, the Russian community is very close. My uncle and the others take pride in their heritage. He doesn't like to speak English at all, and I think he would rather die than be mistaken for anything but a Russian."

Ki shook his head. "But you don't have an accent at all."

"My mother was a teacher," she said gently. "I speak Russian, English, French—also Tlingit and Aleut."

"And your father?" He caught Natalia's expression and raised an apologetic hand. "Hey, I'm sorry. I ask too many questions."

"No, it's all right," she said quickly. "It's just that I don't remember him very well. He died when I was quite young."

From the tone of her voice, it was clear to Ki that this was a subject she didn't care to pursue. She went on to tell him that her mother had died of pneumonia when she, Natalia, was fifteen and that her father's brother, Nikolai, had taken her in and raised her.

"It was very hard for him," she said warmly. "He never married and he knows nothing about children. I'm sure having me in the house has been the most trying experience of his life." She looked up at Ki. "I saw your face back there in the store. You thought he was being too hard on me, I know."

"I saw a man who seems to anger very quickly," Ki answered.

"He loves me, I know that," she sighed. "But he is not a man who would let himself show it." She hesitated a moment, staring out at Sitka Sound. The misty rain was rapidly turning to fog. "Pride is my uncle's sin," she told Ki, "and his downfall as well, I'm afraid. The Shelikhov name is a famous one, you know. I was named for the wife of the great explorer and trader, Gregory Shelikhov. He ruled a trading empire that stretched across the Pacific. But that was a hundred years ago. I am afraid the Shelikhovs are not very important anymore."

"You can't blame a man for being proud of his heritage," said Ki.

"He remembers too much that no longer matters," Natalia said bitterly. "His family was rich and respected. He is a store-keeper. It is hard for him to forget."

Ki took a deep breath. "Natalia," he said carefully, "if an Indian didn't kill Platte, can you tell me who did?"

The girl seemed to stiffen beside him. "My uncle was right," she said coolly, "I should never have spoken of that. It is no concern of mine."

"Maybe not, but it matters a lot to me," Ki persisted. "I have to know, Natalia. I—"

"There is nothing more to say," she snapped, "nothing!" For an instant, her gaze met his. There was anger there, but

15

not for him. Ki saw the touch of fear in the glacier-blue eyes was very real.

"I must get back," she said quickly, "I have work to do."

"Natalia, listen to me." Ki grasped her shoulders and turned her around to face him. "Don't be afraid to talk to me. Please. If you're afraid of something or someone, maybe I can help."

"Help?" Natalia gave him a chilling little laugh and threw off his hands. "Is that why you and the woman came to Alaska—to help my Uncle Nikolai? Tell me, did you bring the American army with you, Ki? Funny, I didn't see them get off the steamer."

Ki watched the girl intently. "Is that what you think you need, Natalia, an army? My God, what kind of trouble have you got up here?"

Natalia flushed and turned away. "My uncle is right again. I talk without thinking."

"Uh-uh. I think you know exactly what you're saying."

"Think what you like," she said stiffly, "it certainly doesn't matter to me!"

Her anger, the defiant set of her mouth, made her all the more desirable to Ki. He wanted to take her in his arms, press those lovely lips to his own. "I think it does matter," he told her. "I think Hiram Platte's murder has a lot to do with whatever's troubling you and your uncle. You know what's going on here in Sitka—don't tell me you don't."

"I don't know what you're talking about." She turned away, refusing to meet his eyes.

"Look, I already know what's happening here," he said firmly. "I know ships are being sunk and that warehouses and buildings somehow mysteriously catch fire. I know the people who built this country—men like your uncle—are being frightened out of business."

Natalia looked at her hands. "I know nothing of things like that."

"What about a man called Kodiak Burke?" Ki said suddenly. "I don't suppose you've heard of him." He saw at once the words had struck home. Natalia's eyes widened in alarm; the thin line of her mouth contorted in fear.

"Leave me alone—please." Her voice was a harsh, desperate whisper.

"Natalia—"

"Aren't you listening to me," she cried out, "I don't know anything, I don't know anything at all!" Her blue eyes flared in anger and she turned on her heels and fled. Ki started after her, then stopped. He watched her slim figure disappear in a thick curtain of fog.

Natalia had tried to hide it, but her eyes had given her away. Burke was more than a name. She was frightened of the man because she knew him. Somehow, he was a very real threat—to her, personally, or to her uncle.

Ki suddenly went rigid. A chill, a silent warning, touched the edge of his mind. Instinctively, his body dropped into a fighting crouch, legs bent slightly at the knees, hands held well away from his sides. He could see nothing at all in the dense gray world around him, hear nothing but the silence. It was *kime*, the samurai sense without a name, that told him they were there. Four of them—three ordinary men, and one not ordinary at all, one with such a sickness in his soul that Ki recoiled from the mental touch, withdrew his mind as if a sliver of ice had pierced his heart.

He moved a step forward and then stopped, going nearly to the ground. Ahead, the four suddenly appeared before his eyes. They were there for an instant, then gone, wraiths swallowed up in the fog. Still, they were visible long enough—Ki saw all he needed to see. The foe he'd sensed so strongly was enormous, a giant of a man. God, he had to be seven feet or more!

They weren't after him, Ki knew. They were moving off north, farther up the street. Ki followed, keeping to the cover of the fog. Something solid loomed up before him. He reached out and touched the wooden edge of a building, paused, and moved cautiously ahead. *They're there . . . just ahead . . . very close now.*

Ki stopped again, then blindly crept forward a few yards. A slight breeze caught the fog and swept it aside. Ki clenched his fists and froze. He saw the dim letters over Shelikhov's store. Once more, the cold presence of his enemy reached out to touch him. He moved quickly, racing for the door that now stood open to the fog. Shelikhov's deep, angry voice reached his ears. A split second later, Natalia's high-pitched scream erased every other sound from his mind.

Chapter 3

Ki came swiftly through the door without a sound, paused a split second, and took in the scene in a glance. Two men— one pressing Natalia's uncle against the wall, the other flailing at his face with both fists. The third man and the giant were nowhere in sight. They had the girl, then, through the door behind the counter.

Ki moved in a blur, his body parallel to the ground. His right foot lashed out hard and caught the first man just below the small of his back. The man screamed, arched like a bow and came up on his toes. Ki tossed him roughly aside, saw the startled expression of the man holding Shelikhov's arms. Ki grabbed his collar and jerked him off the floor. His left hand whipped out in a knife-edge chop. The man's eyes glazed and he dropped limply from Ki's grasp. Shelikhov's eyes darted crazily past Ki. Too late, Ki heard the boot scrape behind him, sensed the blow coming. He twisted frantically aside and felt white-hot pain explode in his shoulder. He hit the floor and rolled, came to his knees, and saw a man's face split in a grin as he swung an iron pipe past his shoulders.

Ki lowered his head and came off the floor with all the strength he could muster. The weapon whispered past his ear. Ki hit the man in the belly with his shoulder, driving him back across the room. The man grunted, swallowed a curse, dropped the pipe, caught his balance, and pounded Ki's head with his fists. Ki spat blood, staggered back, and shook his head to clear his vision. The man came at him like a bull. Ki stood his ground, ducked as the other flailed out with his fists. He came up inside the man's guard with two swift, savage blows to the face. The man stumbled, paused to get his bearings. Ki's stiffened hands moved like pistons, darting in to punish flesh and bone. The man's nose snapped; blood fountained from his nostrils and spilled into his mouth. Ki hit him once more and saw the dark eyes glaze.

He was past the man and moving before his body hit the floor.

"Natalia!" Ki shouted out the name as he raced for the entry behind the curtain. Suddenly, a great headless body filled the door. Ki stopped in his tracks and stared. The body ducked and grew a head. The giant looked at Ki, grinned, and came straight at him. Ki reached out, grabbed the axe handle Natalia had left on the counter and swung it as hard as he could. The blow caught the giant solidly in the belly. He bellowed, stepped back, rubbed his stomach, and then lurched around the counter. One big hand swept out and sent a dozen lamp chimneys flying. Glass shattered against the wall.

Christ! Ki's throat went dry. The blow would have felled a grizzly, and the bastard was still on his feet! Ki backed up, hefting the wooden handle in both hands. The giant discovered his companions on the floor, studied them a moment, and looked questioningly at Ki.

Ki backed slowly toward the store's front door. There was no doubt in his mind—this monster would probably kill him in the close confines of the store. He needed room to move around. Outside, he could put his speed and training to work, keep out of the giant's way. If those tree-sized arms ever caught him . . .

Damp tendrils of fog whirled around him. The giant ducked under the low front door, his big frame filling the narrow space. He was dressed in tight black trousers and a shirt with flowing sleeves buttoned close to his bull-like neck. His head was completely hairless, shaped like the point of a bullet. Skin the color of dirty granite stretched tightly across his skull. Small, pitlike eyes were nearly lost under the bony ridge of his brow. His nose was crushed flat, his mouth a bloodless scar that slit his face.

You're not real pretty, Ki thought soberly, *but you're a big son of a bitch!*

For an instant, fog rolled in to mask the giant in a curtain of gray. Ki bent low and darted quickly to his right. The fog was a silent ally and he was grateful for its presence. He shifted the axe handle from one hand to the other, thrust his right in the pocket of his jacket, and palmed two *shuriken* throwing stars. The man was enormous, but the razor-edge steel was blind to size. Ki knew what he had to do. Stopping the man without killing him was clearly out of the question. A creature like that wasn't down until he was dead.

Ki stopped and turned slowly in a circle, bringing all his senses to bear. He slipped off his jacket to free his arms and dropped the garment quietly to the ground. The man was close, off to his left. Ki took one silent step forward and then another. The *shuriken* was poised in his outstretched hand. *Get it done quickly, bring him down . . . the first steel star to the heart, the next to the cluster of veins in the throat . . .*

Suddenly, the big form appeared; shadow took shape out of the fog. Ki's legs bent at the knees—his arm swept back for the throw that would still the giant's life in an instant. Fog shifted and swirled and filled his vision. The giant faded back and disappeared.

Ki cursed under his breath. He moved quickly away, circling the spot where the man had vanished. In his mind's eye he saw the damp street, the houses, and buildings pressed tightly together. He sensed where the giant would appear, saw him already there. His hand swayed like the head of a snake, wrist slightly bent, the deadly *shuriken* poised and ready. There—

21

off to the right! He had to be there, back toward the edge of the street. When he appeared he'd be nearly facing Ki, his body presenting a target that th—

The giant rose up out of nowhere, came off the ground like a stone splitting the earth. Ki desperately twisted aside, jerked back his arm to loose his weapon. A ham-sized fist struck his chest, lifted him off the street, and sent him flying. The throwing stars fell from his hand. Ki hit hard, came to his knees, and shook his head. He gasped for breath and cried out at the searing pain. *Get up, get up now or you're finished.*

Ki heard the deep bellow of anger and threw himself to the right. A boot grazed his shoulder and Ki dropped to his belly, rolled, and came to his feet. His legs threatened to buckle. Bile rose to his throat and white lights whirled in his head. He knew the whisper of death had brushed his soul. Only a split second of motion had moved him from the center of the strike, a blow that would have driven splintered bone into his heart.

The giant circled him warily, moving like a ghost out of the fog. Ki let him come, watching the hooded eyes, the way he moved his arms and legs. The giant took two steps forward, lifted his hands, and opened his fingers before his chest. Suddenly, he feinted to the left, slammed his foot hard against the ground, and launched himself at Ki from the right. Ki knew the blow was coming—the big fist hammered empty air. Ki jerked his head aside and ducked under a massive shoulder, twisted, and came off the ground. His foot lashed out and caught the giant solidly in the throat.

The man roared in anger, staggered back, and swayed in a dizzy circle. Ki came in low, leaped in the air, and kicked out savagely again, driving his foot hard in the big man's groin. The giant doubled in pain. In one swift motion, Ki's hand whipped out in a wedge toward the base of the giant's nose, a blow that would drive bone and cartilage into the brain. Suddenly, the giant moved in a blur. Ki's hand glanced off of an iron-hard skull. Massive arms closed tightly around his chest, forcing the breath from his body. Ki kicked out desperately, pounding the bearlike body with his knees. Pain screamed in every muscle and tendon. The giant lifted him over his head and hurled him to the ground. Ki twisted frantically, hit on the point of his shoulder, and came awkwardly to his knees. The big man was on him in an instant. His foot struck Ki in the head, driving him to the dirt. Ki threw himself aside, took two steps, and fell on his face. He tried to move but nothing worked. His arms and legs no longer seemed attached to his body. The giant loomed above him. Through a haze of red, Ki saw the massive foot leave the ground, poised for a killing blow to his face.

Sound exploded through the fog and the giant stumbled back and clutched his arm. Another shot blasted through the mist and then another. The giant backed off and stared, looked once at Ki, and turned and vanished.

Ki forced himself up on his arms, blinked, and saw the girl. She held the pistol straight out from her body, gripping it stiffly in both hands. Her hands shook and her eyes were wide with fear.

"Ki, Ki?" She called his name again and again, unable to move or take her eyes off the gray wall of fog.

"It's all right," Ki told her. "He's gone, Natalia. It's all right." He gritted his teeth against the pain, forcing himself to his knees. He tried to stand, pressing his hands firmly against the earth. Nausea struck him like a blow. He fell back, caught himself, and tried again.

"Oh my God, Ki!" She bent to help him, suddenly aware that he was hurt. She gripped his shoulders with strong hands while he brought himself to his feet.

"I'm okay," he told her. "Just give me a hand back to the store. Need to—sit down a minute."

"Can you make it all right? Are you sure?"

"I'll make it," he said tightly. He spotted his jacket on the ground. The girl bent to pick it up. "I'm glad you showed up when you did. You've got real good timing."

"I've never even fired the thing before in my life," she said. "I don't know if I hit him or not."

"You hit him," he assured her. "Enough to scare him off."

"I wish I had killed him," Natalia said darkly. "It is a terrible thing to say, but I wish my bullet had struck him dead!"

Ki was startled by the sudden change in her voice, the intense look of hatred in her eyes. "Who is he, Natalia? What did he want with you and your uncle?"

Natalia took a breath and let it go. "His name is Maksutova. He is Russian. He comes from the north of Alaska, the Kuskokwim River. He--he has a quarrel with my uncle." The words rushed out so quickly, Ki knew it was a lie.

"You're all right? He didn't hurt you, did he? I knew he had you back in that room, I tried to reach you."

"Me?" She looked almost startled at the question. "No, no, he wouldn't hurt me." She turned away, warding off the puzzlement in his eyes. *Now what the hell is that supposed to mean?* He could press her for an answer, but knew he'd be wasting his time. Natalia's manner had told him so in advance.

There were half a dozen men in the store, grim, bearded men with stolid Russian faces. Ki guessed they were Shelikhov's friends. They glanced up at Ki expressionless. Two of the men he'd fought were gone. He doubted if they'd left without help and guessed some of the men here had taken them out. *And done what with them?* he wondered. He had a good idea they'd done nothing at all. One of his assailants lay silent under a blanket. As Ki and Natalia entered, two of the Russians lifted him up and carried him out the front door.

Nikolai sat in a chair, pressing a wet cloth to his cheek. His face was splotched with red. "I am ashamed," he said solemnly. "I have treat you badly, I think. You return my bad manners by coming back to help us."

"I'm just glad you're all right," said Ki.

Shelikhov's dark brows came together in a frown. "You fight Maksutova, *da?*"

"I fought at him," Ki said. "He did a little better than I did."

"If you are alive, you did well," Shelikhov said flatly. "Natalia, this man is hurt. See to him, girl."

"No, I'm fine," Ki protested. "If there's any trouble, I can have a doctor look me over."

Shelikhov laughed. He turned and spoke rapidly in Russian. The men behind him grinned and laughed with him. "The doctor in Sitka, he is a butcher. Worse when he is sober." He waved Ki off with a gruff gesture. "Go now. And give him one of my shirts, Natalia. A good one, mind you—not the one with patches." Shelikhov turned away to speak with his friends.

"You'd better do as he wants," Natalia smiled. "He'll be angry at me if you don't."

"I don't want to put you to any trouble."

"Come on," she said, lowering her chin and giving a fair imitation of her uncle, "I help you, *da?* Give you fine new shirt."

Ki laughed and followed the girl out of the store into the fog.

The house was several blocks up the hill, a square, two-story structure that reminded Ki of the store itself. It was sturdy and well finished, and he guessed Nikolai Shelikhov had built both of the buildings himself.

Natalia led Ki through a narrow hall into the parlor. Ki had never seen a Russian home, and he felt as if he had walked into a completely alien world. The furniture was dark and heavy, the lines unfamiliar. There was a bookcase of worn leather volumes, the titles in gold Cyrillic characters. An enormous brass samovar sat on a table between the kitchen and the parlor. A gold icon held a place of honor on the wall.

Natalia caught Ki's expression and grinned. "Uncle Nikolai says it is exactly like his grandfather's room in St. Petersburg. I don't know how he knows this, since he has never been to Russia—but he swears that it is true."

"I won't argue with him," said Ki.

"Sit down," Natalia ordered, "and take off your shirt. No, that's a waste of time," she sighed. "I'll cut it off. There is nothing left worth saving, and it will hurt you to try to move."

Ki waited while the girl disappeared into the kitchen. In a moment, she returned with a large pair of scissors, hot water, and a neat stack of flannel cloth. He didn't speak until she had deftly cut the strips of the shirt away and tossed them aside. He saw her bite her lip, heard the sharp intake of breath as she discovered the ugly bruise, spreading like a dark purple bloom across his chest. She inspected the small gash on the side of his head, cleaned it, and applied a dab of something that smelled. She washed his chest and shoulders with a warm cloth, being careful not to hurt him.

Ki was keenly aware of the soft touch of her hands against his skin. He could smell the heady perfume of her body, feel her breath upon his shoulder. She bound the strips of flannel about his chest and tied them securely.

"Is that all right? How does it feel?"

"Tight. But that's the way it's supposed to be. You're very good at this."

"Well, of course, I am." She laughed and folded the extra piece of flannel. "Besides, you heard Uncle Nikolai. You don't have any choice. The doctor here is a butcher. That's the truth, I'm afraid."

"Then I'm lucky to be under your care."

Something in his voice made her look right at him. Their eyes met for an instant; Natalia flushed and turned away.

Ki took a breath and pulled himself erect, stood for a moment, and walked to the kitchen. The girl was facing the far wall. She whirled around as he touched her shoulders, startled to find him there. Her mouth opened wide; her eyes darted about like a frightened bird's. His fingers circled her waist and she let out a breath and came against him. She closed her eyes and lifted her face to his.

"Uncle Nikolai will kill us both if he finds us here," she whispered, "you know that, don't you?"

"A man can only come close to death once a day," Ki told her. "I am safe until tomorrow."

Chapter 4

The girl hadn't spoken since they had left the kitchen. Now, she stood in the circle of his arms, keeping her silence and touching him with her eyes. In the half light from the window, the cool azure shade of her eyes turned a deep and smoldering blue, circles so immense, so warm and inviting, Ki could see little else. His hands slid up her arms, past her shoulders and her throat to her cheeks. He gently kissed her eyes, the soft and downy circle before her ears. Natalia's lips went slack. With a sigh, she brought her mouth up hungrily to meet his own. Ki explored the honeyed warmth, letting his tongue caress each small and secret hollow. Natalia trembled like some frightened forest creature. Ki let his lips trail past her cheeks to the graceful column of her throat. A vein pulsed rapidly in her neck. His hands found the circle of her waist, the lovely curve of her back. When his fingers brushed lightly against her breasts, Natalia went limp in his arms and fell against him. Her whole body seemed to shudder; her eyes touched his with wonder, then closed under a thick veil of lashes. When his fingers touched the first pearl button at her throat, her eyes opened quickly and she pressed her hands gently against his chest.

"No, wait, wait..." she whispered. "I–I want to do that. I want to show myself to you..."

Ki said nothing. Her words aroused him, heightened his growing excitement. Natalia stepped back and raised her hands to her bodice. Her fingers opened the buttons one by one. Her dark, luminous eyes never left Ki's. She paused when the buttons were free to her waist. Ki stared at the narrow taper of flesh, the first inviting hint of the swell of her breasts. A slight blush of color darkened the hollows of her throat. Natalia crossed her hands before her breasts, slid her fingers under the fabric at her shoulders, and brought her hands slowly down her arms. Ki's throat went dry. Natalia showed him a lazy, knowing smile, reading the surprise on his features as he saw she wore nothing underneath. She let the cloth fall free and set her palms flat against her waist. The dress hung precariously on the gentle swell of her hips. The motion of her hands arched her shoulders, thrusting the taut, rosy peaks of her breasts at a jaunty angle, hollowing the honeyed flesh beneath her ribs. She cupped her breasts gently in her hands, letting the tips of her fingers tease her nipples into hard little buds. The touch of her own skin brought her pleasure; her head fell back on her shoulders and a sigh escaped her lips.

"Do you want to come to me now," she asked softly. "Do you want to touch me, Ki?"

"I never wanted anything more in my life," Ki said hoarsely. He took a quick step forward. Natalia backed away.

"No. Not yet." She gave him an impish grin, touching the tip of her tongue against her lips. "Wait, Ki. Wait..."

Ki felt his swollen member pressing hard against his trousers. Natalia stroked her hands across her hips and let her dress fall in a froth about her ankles. Stepping out of the fallen garment, she stretched on the tips of her toes and brought her hands to the top of her head. Ki heard the faint clatter of pins against the hardwood floor. Natalia shook her head and fluffed her fingers through her hair. The tight coils at her temples sprang free, tumbling in a veil past her shoulders, kissing the tips of her breasts and brushing the curve of her waist. Natalia laughed and twirled in a little circle, stopped, and grinned at Ki through a dark and tousled mist.

"Do you like it?" she asked. "Do you like my hair, Ki?"

"I like everything about you," Ki said dryly. "My God, Natalia!"

"I wanted to do that," she whispered. "I think I wanted to give myself to you from the moment you looked at me the way you did in the store."

Ki grinned. "You mean when I was trying to buy an axe handle."

"Yes! Lord, I knew exactly what you wanted!" She stretched her arms wide and tossed the long wings of hair across her shoulders. "Now, Ki, take what you want," she cried out, "everything! I give it to you!"

Ki came to her and took her in his arms. He bent to kiss her breasts and Natalia gasped, tightening her fingers in his hair and pressing him close against her. He drew the coral buds past his lips again and again, sucked the silken tips as Natalia's slender form shook with delight. He feasted on the musky taste of her flesh, stroked the hard and dimpled points until they flushed with the bright glow of scarlet.

"Give me your mouth," she demanded, "I want to taste myself on your lips!" Strong, small hands pressed his cheeks, bringing his mouth up to meet her own. Her tongue thrust hungrily past his lips, drinking in the sharp flavor of her nipples. The taste of her own flesh left her gasping, trembling in his arms. Ki took her hand and led her to the bed in the corner. Natalia came eagerly, reached the bed before him, and perched on the edge, holding both his hands as he stood above her. Ki reached for his buckle and her fingers pushed him aside. She loosened his belt, grasped the tops of his denims, and slid them quickly down his legs.

"Oh Lord," she sighed. "Oh, Ki!" Her eyes went wide at the sight of his erection. She gazed at the rigid member; the pink tip of her tongue flicked absently over her lips. Ki leaned forward to join her on the bed. Natalia touched his thigh and stopped him.

"You're hurt," she said, "I don't want you to strain anything."

"I'm not *that* hurt," Ki assured her.

"Maybe," she said solemnly, "but I don't want to take any chances. The best thing for you to do is relax and take it easy."

"What?" Ki stared at the girl in alarm. "Natalia, the last thing I want to do right now is take it easy!"

"Now you don't know that, do you? You just might." Natalia laughed, reached up to grasp his shoulders, and pressed him easily down on the bed. "You see? It is all right to relax. This way, you will not need the muscles in your chest."

"Yeah," Ki said hoarsely, "you're right."

Her moist lips opened and her tongue flicked out to flutter gently over his shaft. Ki felt himself swell at her touch. She pressed two fingers about him and held him straight, grinned like a cat, then took his length into her mouth.

Ki went rigid and clenched his fists. Hot points of fire engulfed his loins. Natalia's hands clutched hungrily at his thighs; her head moved in a slow, lazy circle above his belly. A mist of dark hair caressed his flesh, burning him like a brand. Again and again, Natalia stroked him with the furnace of her mouth. Her throat made tiny sounds of delight as she kneaded him with her lips. Her tongue slid softly along the underside of his member; her cheeks went hollow as she sought to draw him deeper and deeper into her mouth.

Ki let a ragged whisper of pleasure pass through his teeth. The pressure in his loins swelled to bursting. An agony of pain and delight stretched every cord and tendon in his body. Natalia's practiced tongue darted over him like a snake. Once, she raised her head and looked right at him. The flashing blue eyes glowed with a fierce and wanton pleasure. She teased him, releasing him until he could scarcely feel the heat of her breath. Her lips encircled the sensitive head of his shaft, sucking the tender flesh until Ki was ready to come out of his skin. He hung suspended on the high crest of delight, only a touch from joyous release. Natalia refused to let him go. She pushed him over the edge, drew him back, stroked him intently, then held him off again.

Ki felt the storm raging within him, racing through his body. Still, Natalia held him, a long, agonizing moment that seemed to last forever. Ki was certain that his body would explode, shatter in a thousand orgasms at once. Natalia sensed his excitement and raked deep furrows along his thighs. Ki cried out at her touch.

Suddenly, Natalia's mouth moved in a frenzy; she drew him deeply within her until her brow slammed hard against his belly.

Lightning struck Ki's loins with a heat that made him shudder. Natalia groaned as he exploded again and again into her mouth. He filled her with his warmth, one thunderous surge after another. Natalia refused to let him go. She circled his thighs with her arms and ground her mouth savagely against him.

Ki relaxed and went limp. For a long moment, Natalia nestled between his legs, sleepily draining the last bit of pleasure from his loins. Finally, Ki reached down and drew her into the hollow of his arms. Natalia moaned and settled herself against him, one long leg draped languorously over his thigh.

"That was some kind of loving," Ki told her. "My God, Natalia—you damn near killed me!"

"You are satisfied with me, *da?*"

Ki laughed at her thick Russian accent. "Yeah, you might say I'm satisfied. For the moment."

She peered up at him. "For the moment, is it? And just what is that supposed to mean?"

"It means you had a real nice surprise for me. Now I've got one for you."

"Ha! Men always have to brag. You *will* have a surprise for me sometime. I do not think you have one now."

"Give me a few minutes and I'll show you."

"Your brag is quite safe, I'm afraid." She gave a deep sigh of regret and pulled herself erect. "You won't *be* here in a few minutes, Ki. You must go. Really." Her eyes touched his with resignation. "I mean it. You must leave quickly. I assure you, Uncle Nikolai will know how long it should take to see to your wounds and find you a shirt. If he should decide to see for himself..."

31

"Right." The warning in her eyes was clear enough. Confronting Nikolai Shelikhov, naked and in bed with his niece, was a moment he could easily do without. He grabbed the bedpost and pulled himself straight, biting his lips against the stiffness in his chest. Slipping quickly into his trousers, he thrust his arms gingerly into the shirt Natalia brought him. When he turned, he was surprised to see Natalia fully dressed. She whipped her long hair atop her head, then covered it with a scarf tied under her chin. She caught Ki's look and rolled her eyes.

"I know. I doubt if I'd fool a blind man, much less my uncle."

"You don't look exactly prim and proper."

"I *look* as if I just got out of bed with you," she said ruefully. "If you'll get out of here now, I'll try to repair some of the damage."

"I don't want to run into your uncle," Ki said evenly, "but I don't want to leave you, either. What I want to do is get you back in that bed. Right now."

Natalia closed her eyes and caught her breath. "Don't—don't talk like that," she said shakily. "God, you don't know what it does to me. Down—down there." She touched her hand lightly between her legs.

"I know what it does to me."

"Oh, Ki!" She gave a little cry and ran swiftly into his arms. Her mouth opened to his like a flower. She clung to him hungrily, pressing the full length of her body against his own. His hands found the lush curve of her bottom, the deep cleft between her hips. Natalia gasped and pulled away, her face flush with color.

"Stop that *now*," she trembled, "while I—while I still have the strength to get you out of here." She clasped his hand firmly and led him down the narrow stairs through the parlor. She kissed him quickly at the door, then backed away.

"Soon," she told him. "I'll find a way. I promise."

"You'd better," he said solemnly.

"Get out of here," she said, "right now." She opened the door and pressed him playfully onto the porch. The door clicked shut behind him.

Ki sniffed the air and let his eyes dart quickly down the street. The fog was gone, turned once more to a light misting rain. He breathed a sigh of relief. The fog would give him cover, but it would do the same for others—men who might decide to finish the job they'd started. For the moment, he had no desire to tangle with anyone else—midgets, giants, or any size in between.

Turning a corner quickly, he saw a man standing in front of the alley. He was a broad-shouldered Indian with tangled hair and flat, wooden features. His clothes were worn and faded, trade clothes that clearly didn't fit. Ki met the man's eyes and knew at once the Indian had been watching, waiting for him to appear. His dark eyes were intense, expectant, as if he were trying to decide what to do. He held Ki's gaze another moment, then turned and disappeared down the alley.

Ki stopped, instinctively patting the pocket of his jacket, suddenly remembering the two *shuriken* throwing stars were somewhere back in the street before the store, knocked from his hand when the giant had come out of the fog. He muttered under his breath and walked on. Whatever the man wanted, it apparently wasn't a fight. That suited Ki just fine.

Jessie stared at the window a long moment, then turned abruptly and faced Ki again. Her features were drawn in concern, green eyes flecked with brooding anger.

"Damn it all," she flared, "Kodiak Burke's behind this business somewhere. I can't prove it, but I can feel it!"

"The girl and her uncle both know the Indian didn't kill Platte," Ki told her. "That's no big secret in Sitka."

"It's no big secret, but no one talks about it, either."

"Exactly. I know what you're thinking, Jessie. Burke wields the power here and no one wants to cross him. Natalia never said Burke was behind Platte's death. But she turned white as a sheet when I brought up his name."

"This business you walked in on," Jessie said thoughtfully, "the giant—what's his name?"

"Maksutova."

"Yes, Maksutova. Do you have any idea what that was all about?"

33

"Natalia says he has some kind of quarrel with her uncle."

"And you said you don't believe her."

"I don't. She's hiding something, but I have no idea what it is—" Ki stopped and gave Jessie a curious look. He knew Jessie Starbuck well; he was alert to the slight intonations of her voice, a sudden change in her expression. "You're trying to tie Burke into what happened at the store. How are you going to do that?"

"I'm not trying to do anything," she said evenly. "I'm just wondering, is all."

"About what?"

"This Nikolai Shelikhov has a business in Sitka, Ki. He wouldn't be the first merchant Kodiak Burke has tried to drive out of town."

Ki frowned and shook his head. "Maybe. I don't think so, Jessie. It isn't much of a store. I'd guess Shelikhov's pride is all that's keeping the door open. I don't think Burke and the cartel would bother. They're after bigger game."

Jessie shrugged, walked to her dresser, and poured them both a brandy. "Still, I'd like to meet Shelikhov and his niece. It's a start, and we don't have a lot of friends in this town."

"We can go in the morning if you like."

"Good." Jessie set her brandy on the table and glanced at Ki. He was looking into his drink, slumped down wearily in his chair. "You're all right, aren't you?" she asked. "Is there anything I can do?"

"I'll be okay," he assured her. "I need a good night's sleep is all."

"Uh-huh. And a couple of days in a hospital wouldn't hurt."

"Jessie, I'm *fine*."

She poured him another brandy. Ki was no drinker, but this time he didn't refuse. He downed the glass quickly, made a face, and set it aside.

"Go to bed," Jessie told him. "We'll walk down to the store in the morning. I've got to stop by Hiram Platte's office; I'm sure there's nothing there that'll help but it has to be done. You want anything to eat tonight?"

"No, I'm not hungry. All I want is sleep." He pulled himself painfully erect and moved to the door.

"Ki . . ."

He turned and saw her leaning against the wall, hands folded over her breasts. "Ki, I told you about Joshua Gray because I thought you ought to know. I saw your face when I told you what happened. Don't, Ki."

"Don't what?"

"Don't go after him. And *please* don't tell me the thought never crossed your mind. He's not going to bother me again."

"You know that, do you?" Ki said darkly.

"I think I do." She saw the scowl deepening between his brows and forced a laugh. "Tell you what. If you won't go after Joshua Gray, I promise I won't run out and shoot this Maksutova."

Ki opened the door and gave her a long solemn look. "If you get a chance," he said flatly, "I'd recommend a Sharps buffalo gun—right through the head at two feet."

Chapter 5

For a long time after Ki returned to his room, Jessie lay in darkness, turning restlessly on the uncomfortable bed. She wondered idly what the malodorous, hard mattress contained. Horseshoes, certainly—railroad spikes and nails for good measure. For a moment she considered trying the floor. She had spent many nights sleeping soundly outdoors with no more than a blanket and a rolled up poncho for a pillow. You could pick your own spot outside, smooth out the lumps, and get some sleep. There was no such luxury at the Grande Pacific Hotel.

When sleep finally found her, the storm brought her quickly awake. Rain lashed the glass panes and thunder shook the clapboard walls. With a sigh Jessie slipped out of bed and padded wearily to the window. Lightning seared the tiny room, painting her naked flesh harsh white and shadow. She stared into the night. The storm that howled above her now had been born far out in the northern Pacific, maybe a thousand miles away. Her father had told her stories of such storms, of the awesome *tai-fung*, the Great Wind, and how it churned through the China Sea and wreaked havoc upon the Japans.

It began there, with him . . . it began before I was born and now it has brought me here.

Ki believed life was an intricately woven tapestry, its many-colored threads stretching unbroken across the years. If that were so, then she was truly a part of the pattern that her father had begun. Alex Starbuck had carved a trading empire for himself, starting with the newly opened ports of the Japans. There, he had run afoul of a wealthy Prussian business cartel, ruthless men determined to make their fortunes in the Orient. Not content with only a share of the treasures to be gained, they struck out at any who challenged their supremacy in the Pacific. Alex Starbuck stood in their way—he was a proud, stubborn man who meant to keep what he'd worked so hard to gain.

The cartel struck, and Starbuck struck back. Finally, the fight raged across Europe and America. Jessie's mother was murdered, and finally the faceless men killed Alex himself on his own Texas ranch. Jessie inherited the vast Starbuck holdings, and the terrible legacy that went with them. The choice to walk away or stand and fight had never crossed her mind. Jessie was Alex Starbuck's daughter.

She and Ki had met the cartel's threats more than once. They struck without warning, determined to gain control of the nation's political and financial seats of power. The tools of their trade were murder, bribery, coercion, and extortion. Jessie knew from experience that they would stop at nothing to reach their goals. She was well aware that Alaska could be the biggest, most lucrative coup the cartel had ever attempted. Fools still called the place Walrussia and Seward's Folly, but intelligent, enterprising men knew better. There were untold riches in the land—countless acres of timber, rich land for farming, gold, and hints of more to come.

Yet, this enormous land was nearly empty. Jessie had been appalled to learn there were 30,000 Indians or more in Alaska—and fewer than 450 whites, most of those crowded into Sitka and Wrangell. Over half a million square miles ripe for the taking. The cartel wouldn't have to fight for Alaska—nobody else even wanted the place!

Jessie let out a breath and turned away from the window.

The storm was drifting away, hurling itself against the inland mountains. If Kodiak Burke and the cartel wanted Alaska, who was going to stop them? Jessie Starbuck and Ki? There were no soldiers, no marshals—not even a town constable within a thousand miles. Only a handful of naval officers to hold down the fort. Jessie laughed aloud. "God, yes—like Lieutenant Joshua Gray. Now there's a man who'll help us save Alaska!"

As Jessie'd expected, there was nothing of interest in Hiram Platte's office. His clerk had left Sitka before Platte was in the ground, fleeing town without his pay. Jessie didn't have to guess who'd scared him off. The disarray in the office told her someone had taken his time going through Platte's papers.

"Do you think he left anything?" asked Ki. "Anything that would shed more light on what we know about Burke?"

They were walking north away from Sitka Sound, toward Shelikhov's store up the street. Jessie turned and squinted over the blue-green water. "I don't know," she said. "They evidently *thought* Platte wrote something down. Either that, or they just wanted to make sure he didn't." She ran a hand through copper-bright hair. "If we get the time, Ki, we'll try to find someone to put poor Hiram's place in order. If there was a Western Union here, I'd have Murdock in San Francisco send up a replacement."

"When word gets around what happened up here," Ki said ruefully, "you're not going to have a lot of applicants breaking down the door."

Jessie didn't answer. The sun swept shadow off the far inland mountains. A family of Tlingit Indians passed on the street, heading for the salmon works at the waterfront. The man and his wife averted their eyes, staring at the ground. The child, a small boy, gave Jessie a sidelong glance and grinned. The mother caught him at it and shook him soundly back in line.

"Not a real friendly bunch," said Jessie. "Don't guess you can blame 'em, either. This was their island before the Russians took it away from them. A Comanche once told me he spits on the ground every morning just to remind himself it isn't his. Friend, you're not listening to me at all, are you?"

"Huh?" Ki looked up suddenly. "Yes, of course, I am."

"Right." Jessie kept walking. She spoke without turning to Ki. "I think I know you well enough to say this. If I don't, we're in big trouble. I saw how you looked when you came in yesterday. I don't mean your bruises, either. It was there in your eyes, where you and I know each other best. You got whipped and you don't like it. You think it takes something from you, that you're less than you were before."

"People imagine they see things in others," Ki said shortly.

"And it's none of my business."

"That could be. Yes."

"All right. I'm rude and impolite. And you're wrong, Ki. Someone got the better of you. It hasn't happened often. You got through it all right, and if I know you, you learned something. Probably a great deal. If you meet him again it won't happen the same way. You know that's true, Ki. Think about that part. Don't dwell on the other."

Ki kept his silence for a long moment. "Great," he said finally, "that's all I really need."

"What?"

"You—spouting Oriental philosophy. 'The willow does not break. It bends with the wind.'"

Jessie laughed. "What do you expect? I had a good teacher."

"I regret that I ever spoke of such things," Ki said soberly.

When Jessie saw Natalia, she confirmed what she'd suspected after Ki had first spoken of the girl. The things he'd neglected to mention told her all she needed to know. Meeting them at the door of her uncle's store, the tall, slender beauty greeted Jessie warmly, then turned her gaze on Ki. Her enormous blue eyes glowed with delight; the high curves of her cheeks flushed with remembered pleasure. She cordially invited them in, then ran to the rear of the store to find her uncle.

"Ki," Jessie exclaimed, "she's breathtaking! I don't remember you mentioning that at all."

"Oh, didn't I?" Ki's features showed no expression. "Yes, I suppose she is very pretty."

"Pretty . . . Yes, she is. Maybe even attractive. Or moderately presentable."

"All right, Jessie." Ki's face flushed with color.

"What she is," said Jessie, thoroughly enjoying his discomfort, "is one of the most strikingly beautiful women I've ever seen. It's funny you didn't notice."

Ki showed visible relief when Natalia returned with her uncle in tow. He made the introductions and noted Shelikhov's reaction to Jessie. His brows raised in surprise and appreciation; one hand rose unconsciously to straighten his collar.

"I have the honor to greet you," he said solemnly. "Come, please. Natalia—make tea!" Shelikhov ushered them quickly behind the counter and through the door to the back room. It was a storeroom stacked with goods, one small corner reserved for a desk, a worn table, and chairs.

"Well, well now." Shelikhov beamed with pleasure. "You are one of us, then, *da?* A trader, like myself. This is good, very good, I think!"

Natalia served fragrant Japanese tea in delicate cups and saucers. After a moment Jessie set down her cup and looked at Nikolai. "Mr. Shelikhov," she said evenly, "I want to be perfectly honest with you. To do any less would be an affront to your hospitality. I am looking for answers to some very puzzling questions. Ki tells me that you are reluctant to discuss some of the things I need to know. I am asking you, now, to give me permission to question you myself. I will understand and respect your decision to refuse me."

Shelikhov squirmed uneasily in his chair. "Miss Starbuck, I—ah—I would be pleased to help you any way I can. There are reasons, certain things."

"Of course," Jessie said warmly. "If I touch upon something you don't wish to discuss, just say so. Will that be all right?"

"Yes, certainly." Shelikhov forced a smile. "I will help you, yes."

"Will you tell me what you know about Hiram Platte?" Jessie began. "It doesn't seem to be any secret in Sitka that an Indian wasn't the killer."

Shelikhov scowled and looked at his hands. "Is true," he said darkly. "This man Platte, I like him. Everybody know he is good to the Kolosh, the Tlingits. He work sometimes with the people in Wrangell who have a mission there for the Indians.

40

The—who you call them, girl?"

"The Presbyterians," Natalia put in.

"*Da*. The Presby—terians. They run school and mission. Here in Sitka, too. Platte work with them when he can."

Jessie exchanged a quick look with Ki. "He was a friend of the Tlingits? He worked with them?"

"*Da*. This is so."

"That doesn't sound like a man the Indians would choose to murder."

"No. This is true," Shelikhov admitted.

"Who, then?" Jessie asked. "Who would want to kill him?"

Shelikhov's face clouded. "Do you think I would know this? People who do murder do not put a sign upon their door, Miss Starbuck."

"Uncle . . ."

Shelikhov's eyes flashed a warning at his niece. "The tea is cold, Natalia. Get our guests fresh cups, please."

"No, thank you, Natalia." Jessie nodded to the girl and faced her uncle again. "I should not have asked the question, Mr. Shelikhov. It wasn't quite fair because I already know the answer. A man named Kodiak Burke had Hiram Platte murdered. I have no proof of that and don't need any. *I know*. He was murdered because he worked for me. And because he knew things about Burke that Burke and some others don't want me to know."

Shelikhov's eyes widened in alarm. "I don't know of such things," he sputtered. "I have troubles of my own, Miss Starbuck. I am attacked in my own store. You know this. I owe much to Ki here—but I cannot tell you things I do not know!"

"Of course. I understand." Jessie stood, and Shelikhov came to his feet. "Thank you for the tea," Jessie told him, "and forgive the questions, please. I'm going to have to leave you, I'm afraid. Ki, why don't you stay? I'll meet you later at the hotel."

"Yes, certainly," Ki agreed. He caught her silent signal and understood. It was clear she'd gone as far as she could with Shelikhov. Did she really think he could do any better on his own? Ki had his doubts, but he would do as Jessie asked.

41

Shelikhov walked Jessie through the store to the front door. "Miss Starbuck," he said hesitantly, "you think badly of me. I see this. You think Nikolai Shelikhov does not repay the kindness of his friends."

"I think nothing of the sort." Jessie laid a hand on his arm. "I think you are a friend. And Ki and I need friends in Sitka. I wanted the chance to meet you—and I didn't intend to take advantage of your hospitality."

"No, please, you did nothing," Shelikhov insisted. "And you must call me Nikolai. I want you to think of me as friend."

"I do. And for more reasons than one."

"*Da*, yes?"

"Sometimes, friends turn out to have the same enemies. I ask you to think about this."

Shelikhov's eyes betrayed him, and Jessie knew her words had struck home.

"Miss Starbuck—"

"No, nothing need be said," she told him. "Not now. Just remember. Good-bye, Nikolai."

She turned away and walked back down the street, knowing he was standing in the doorway watching her go. It was a wild guess she made about their having the same enemies. Kodiak Burke would have everything nailed down tight on his home ground. A man like Maksutova couldn't run his little strongarm game—or whatever else it might be—without Burke's blessing. Shelikhov knew that, too. Their enemies *were* the same, whether he cared to admit it or not.

The morning was chillier than she'd reckoned, and Jessie wished she'd brought a coat. She hadn't exactly lied to Ki about her destination; she had simply avoided telling him the truth, knowing he wouldn't approve. She intended to go to the waterfront settlement, the slum where the Tlingits lived. If Platte had treated the Indians well, maybe they'd be willing to talk. It was a long shot, certainly, but worth a try at least. And what else was there to do? Walk around Sitka again? Go back to her charming room?

"Miss Starbuck—may I speak to you a moment?"

Jessie stopped as a tall man approached her from the side

of the street. He wore a well-cut plain black suit, a white shirt, and a black string tie. She recognized him at once. His penetrating eyes had met hers as she left the steamer the day before.

"We've met, Miss Starbuck," he told her, "in a manner of speaking."

"In a manner of speaking, we have." Jessie allowed herself a smile. "And you would be . . . ?"

"Marcus Hunter." He touched the brim of his pearl-gray Stetson. "May I walk along with you? I think it's important that we talk."

Jessie raised a brow. She liked the man's attractive, rough-hewn features. "Talk about what, Mr. Hunter?"

"Matters of mutual importance."

"I see."

"That doesn't say a lot, does it?"

"No, not a great deal."

Hunter frowned in thought, working hard at getting his words together. "There are things I need to say. I don't want this to come out wrong and scare you off."

Jessie's green eyes flashed. "I don't scare easily," she said coolly. "Why don't you just try me, Mr. Hunter."

Hunter nodded. "I know a lot about you. I know who you are and that you run the Starbuck holdings. I knew Hiram Platte. Not too well, but well enough. I know for sure an Indian didn't stick that knife in his back."

"I managed to figure that out for myself," Jessie told him.

"Yeah, well, so did everyone else." Hunter paused a moment. "I understand you met Lieutenant Joshua Gray."

The name caught Jessie unaware; she was glad she wasn't looking right at him. "I've met him," she said.

"Your friend—the Oriental—I'm sure he's smart enough to figure this out for himself, but tell him anyway. Maksutova's a bad man to tangle with. He's Kodiak Burke's enforcer—he won't forget your friend, believe me."

Jessie looked curiously at Marcus Hunter. "Who are you, mister?" she demanded. "Just what is it you do here in Sitka?"

"I'm a businessman. I have several different interests in Alaska."

43

"What kind of interests?"

"Trading, mostly. I've got a small piece of one of the salmon outfits in town. I handle some gold interests for people in Portland and San Francisco." Hunter's features spread in a crooked grin. "That isn't really your question, is it? What you want to know is why I'm so concerned with *your* affairs."

"The question had crossed my mind," Jessie said dryly.

"Like I said, I think we share matters of mutual interest."

"Uh-huh. And what sort of matters would those be?"

"I think we should—ah—know each other a little better before we get into that, Miss Starbuck."

"Oh, really?" Jessie showed him a cool and distant smile. "And what makes you think we're going to do that?"

Hunter flushed. "I only meant that you've got a friend here in Sitka if you need one. I'm not asking for your trust. Not now. I just hope that we can—"

Hunter's words were cut short as a bright flash of light seared the sky. A split second later, an earth-shattering sound rent the air. Jessie turned and caught her breath as an invisible hammer of heat touched her face.

"My God, what was that!"

"The harbor," Hunter said tightly, "get down—quick!" He pushed her roughly off her feet and covered her with his body. An instant later, fiery debris began to rain from the overcast sky.

Chapter 6

By the time Jessie and Hunter reached the harbor, a column of black, oily smoke rose three hundred feet into the sky. Flames licked the waters of Sitka Sound, and through the veil of smoke and fire Jessie could see the charred masts of a ship and part of a blackened funnel. Burning chunks of wood had been tossed in every direction. Men swarmed atop the roof of a nearby warehouse, fighting the fire set by a piece of ship's planking.

"If anyone was aboard they're dead now," Hunter muttered under his breath. "Poor bastards."

"What happened?" Jessie asked. "Lord, I never saw such an explosion!"

"Boiler, maybe. Something like that."

Jessie looked sharply at Hunter, wondering why his words seemed to lack conviction. Hunter, though, was looking the other way, watching the men in longboats rowing out to search for bodies.

Jessie turned and saw an open carriage approaching the wharf. The crowd of onlookers gave way to let it pass. Jessie was struck by the fine, matched pair of coal-black mares, the red leather rigging and harness that matched the bright enameled sides of the carriage. The passengers were still too far away for a good look, but she could make out a tall man in a gray suit and gray hat, and the golden hair of a girl beside him.

"Who's that," Jessie asked in wonder, "the mayor himself?"

There was something in Hunter's eyes she couldn't fathom. "That's Kodiak Burke, Miss Starbuck. If you'd like to meet him, I'll introduce you."

"No, I don't think so." Jessie blurted out the words and felt the heat rise to her face. Anger replaced the quick moment of fear she'd experienced at the name. Her green eyes flashed at Hunter. "Yes, I would appreciate that very much," she said tightly. "Mr. Burke is a man I'd like to meet."

Hunter didn't answer. He simply nodded and stalked toward the carriage. Jessie did her best to stay with him, furious at the long-legged strides that made her lift her skirts and scurry like a fool. She could feel Burke's eyes upon her. When she looked up he was smiling, a faint hint of amusement in his eyes.

"Morning, Marcus," he said evenly. "Terrible thing to happen, terrible." His eyes were still locked on Jessie. They were lazy, half-hooded eyes, a rattler taking it easy in the shade.

"Mr. Burke, Miss Jessie Starbuck," said Hunter.

"A pleasure, Miss Starbuck. I heard you were in Sitka."

"Did you?" said Jessie. "How nice."

Burke smiled. Understanding passed between them. He was a stocky man in his forties with the broad, off-center features of a boxer. Scar tissue polished the bony prominence of his brow; his nose had been sketched upon his face over the stubborn thrust of his jaw. Jessie knew the man's features mirrored his past. He was a streetfighter, a cunning and ruthless man who'd slashed his way up through the slums of New York's East Side, then taken his talents west. The fine, English-cut suit did little to hide his beginnings. Many men had overcome such a start, but Kodiak Burke hadn't tried.

"I'm having a few people up to the house this evening," said Burke. "Be sure and drop by, Marcus. And bring Miss Starbuck along with you."

Jessie swallowed her anger. "I'm not with Mr. Hunter," she said coolly. "But thanks just the same, Mr. Burke."

"No offense intended, Miss Starbuck," Burke said smoothly. "The invitation stands. In any form you choose."

"No thanks," Jessie said bluntly. "I'm all tied up."

"We'll miss you," Burke said idly. "Driver." He nodded slightly and the carriage lurched forward. The yellow-haired girl beside him had never looked in Jessie's direction. She was young, barely sixteen if Jessie was right. She had a pretty, porcelain face and vacant blue eyes.

"Your idea to meet him," Hunter said, "not mine."

Jessie turned on him. "Yes, you're right, Mr. Hunter."

"Look, he was the one put the invitation that way. Not me." Hunter shrugged. "I don't guess it makes a lot of difference. I'd guess a party at Kodiak Burke's about the last place you'd be going, considering how—" Hunter caught himself, but the words were already said.

"Considering what, mister?" Jessie's eyes narrowed intently. "Seems to me you know a hell of a lot more about my business than you need to."

Hunter let out a breath. "Miss Starbuck, listen—"

"No, you listen, fella," Jessie said sharply. "Tell your friend Mr. Kodiak Burke I'll be at that party. I just won't be coming with you."

Hunter stared. "I hope you're not serious."

"I am dead serious, mister."

"Don't," Hunter told her. His dark eyes narrowed to slits. "That'd be a fool thing to do. Stay away from Burke!"

"Thanks for the advice," said Jessie. "I don't need it." She turned and stalked off across the wharf.

The carriage she'd hired from the stable rolled through the darkening streets of Sitka. Jessie was surprised to find there were dwellings on the far end of town that weren't gray, weathered, and ready to collapse. The driver took her past neat, two-story clapboards painted white, homes she might have seen in St. Louis or some small Midwestern town. Half a mile farther, the street ended at a high, forbidding iron gate. The gate stood open, and the rutted dirt road became a drive of crushed stone, the only attempt at paving Jessie had seen in all of Sitka. Beyond was the sprawling white house of Kodiak Burke, every window ablaze.

For the first time since she'd left Marcus Hunter that afternoon, Jessie wondered if she'd made a big mistake, if she was walking into something she couldn't handle.

"It's a damn fool thing to do and you know it," Ki had argued. "You are not going to put yourself right in Burke's hands!"

"How much safer am I here in this hotel?" Jessie had asked. "Kodiak Burke makes his own law in Alaska, Ki. He can do anything he wants. If he wants me dead he'll simply send some of his people up the stairs to knock on the door."

"You're making *my* point," Ki said darkly, "not yours."

Now, standing on the edge of the party, the room full of laughing people, Jessie felt a quick moment of panic and desperation. There was no threat or menace in this place, no sense of danger. The scene said Kodiak Burke was holding court, that neither he nor his guests had any doubts that the vast wealth of Alaska was already in his hands. She caught Marcus Hunter staring at her, and shot him an icy smile. *Just want to be friends, do you? You're here, mister, and that tells me who your friends are.*

Jessie had learned an interesting fact from Ki, after he'd returned from Shelikhov's store. Natalia had mentioned Marcus Hunter's name, telling Ki she didn't trust him at all. He came by the store and asked questions, never buying a thing. Jessie wasn't surprised. As she'd already discovered, Hunter was a man who took too much interest in other people's affairs.

My God, they're all here, she thought darkly. Everyone in town toadying up to the winner! There were well-dressed merchants, men of obvious wealth from the States, and a sprinkling of naval officers. She spotted Lieutenant Joshua Gray across the room. He gave her a bleary-eyed look and disappeared.

"Ah, Miss Starbuck, you decided to come. I am delighted."

Jessie turned to face Kodiak Burke, forcing herself to meet the hooded eyes, the satisfied smile that split his features. He wore a well-cut black velvet suit, a burgundy silk vest, and a ruffled ivory shirt. Jessie repressed a shudder, reminding herself this man who looked like an ape dressed up for the circus was as deadly as a viper.

"Did I surprise you, then?" she asked. "You didn't think I'd come?"

"Let's say I admire your nerve," Burke said flatly.

Jessie nodded in understanding. *There's no need for words between us. We both know each other too well.*

"You have a lovely home here," she said idly. "I'm surprised you didn't move into Baranov's Castle on the hill. Maybe put in a tower and a moat."

"What the hell are you doing here?" Burke asked sharply. "What did you think you could accomplish coming to Sitka?"

"I have business interests in Alaska."

"I *know* your business, lady."

"And I *know* yours," Jessie said coolly. She showed him a pleasant smile. "Be careful, Burke. Your Prussian friends pay well, but they don't tolerate mistakes. One is all you'll get."

Burke's face colored with sudden fury. For an instant, the cords in his throat went taut, then he forced himself to swallow his anger. "My home is yours," he said evenly. "Enjoy yourself, Miss Starbuck."

Jessie took a glass of champagne from the tray of one of the liveried Indians circulating among the guests. For an instant, the man's dark and somber eyes met hers, then darted quickly away. Jessie avoided the crowded room and wandered toward the back of the house. A dimly lit hall led to a large timbered room with polished hardwood floors. The large, striking tapestry over the sofa caught Jessie's eyes and held them. It was a flat, almost geometric design, a squarish face with broad, narrow eyes and flattened teeth. The colors were sea-green and the pale ochre cast of the earth.

"It's a Chilkat robe," said Marcus Hunter, "made of mountain goat wool and cedar bark. The Tlingit chiefs wear it in ceremonial dances—or used to, anyway. Not a lot of that going on anymore."

Jessie glanced over her shoulder; he was leaning in the doorway behind her. "Is that what you do here, Mr. Hunter?

49

Guide folks around on the tour?"

Hunter shook his head. "Stop it, Miss Starbuck. You don't know what the hell you're talking about."

"Don't I?"

"No, you don't." He came to her side and studied the robe. "Is that what you think? That I work for Kodiak Burke?"

"Is there anyone here who doesn't—in one way or another?"

"Yeah. Me." He turned suddenly and grasped her bare shoulders, his dark eyes burning into hers. "I don't work for anyone—especially Burke. Believe that, Miss Starbuck!" His voice was harsh and intense, but so low she could scarcely hear him. Jessie pulled away and rubbed her arms.

"If you don't work for him, you sure seem friendly enough. You don't mind me saying, you seem to fit right in here, Mr. Hunter."

"I do. But I've got a good reason." His eyes flicked down the empty hall and back to Jessie.

"And what might that be?"

"Damn it, what are you *doing* in this place," Hunter blurted. "You should never have come into this house!"

Jessie laughed. "You keep doing it, you know? You don't want to answer a question, you just go on to something else."

"Please, don't waste time trying to get the best of me," he said darkly. "I'm not playing some kind of game. You're not safe here. Not even in this crowd. Come on, I'll get you out of here and back to your hotel." He reached for Jessie's arm. Jessie pulled away.

"And I'll be *safe* with you, right?"

"Yes, you will. Please believe that. I'd never—"

"Mr. Hunter," Jessie said suddenly, "why are you so interested in Nikolai Shelikhov? And what does Kodiak Burke want with him? You're so interested in my well-being, give me the answer to that."

The question took Hunter completely by surprise. He stepped back as if Jessie had struck him.

"Good Christ, lady, if Burke even guessed you knew *anything* about that, anything at all—!"

"Anything about what? What does he want with those people? You know, don't you?"

50

"No, there's something. I don't know what," he said tightly. He glanced furtively over his shoulder. "We're leaving—right now. I'm getting you out of here."

"I'm leaving," Jessie told him, "but not with you, friend. I've got a feeling I'd be a lot safer alone."

Hunter made a noise between his teeth. "Don't be a damn fool. You don't have any idea what you're into up here."

"I know exactly what I'm into, Mr. Hunter." Her green eyes flashed a warning. "And *you* stay the hell out of my way."

Jessie turned and left him standing. She stalked down the empty hall, skirted the room full of people, and found the front door. Outside, the sky was dark and clear, ablaze with cold stars of the northern constellations. Jessie hugged her arms, wishing she'd brought a wrap. To her left, horses lazed before a white hitching pole. A dozen carriages crowded together on the crushed rock drive. The drivers were huddled in small groups smoking and talking, waiting for the festivities to end.

"Now, which one's mine?" Jessie muttered under her breath. She tossed back her hair and started walking. The horse was a spotted gelding, she remembered that much. She wondered why Burke didn't keep any people outside; there were plenty of servants in the house.

A man came out of nowhere, a shadow against the dense thicket of hedge that surrounded the house. Jessie started and stepped back.

"No, missa . . ." The man touched a finger to his lips. "Missa Stah-a-book, I talk quick to you, please!"

"What—what do you want, what is it?" Dim starlight touched the man's face and Jessie recognized him at once. He was the Indian from inside, the man who'd served her champagne and looked briefly into her eyes. Now, his eyes darted fearfully in every direction. A band of light striped the flat bridge of his nose, the sharp planes of his cheeks.

"To you . . . I give some-tin. Mistah Platte he say to do this."

Jessie drew in a breath. "Platte? You've got something for me from Hiram Platte?"

"Yes. From the Mistah Platte. He say I must make certain this thing get to you. He say I—" The man broke off abruptly. His eyes darted to Jessie's right and he vanished into the hedge.

51

Jessie turned and saw two men walking quickly toward her from the porch. They made no sound at all, but the Indian had heard them well enough.

"You need some help, lady?" The taller of the two stepped forward, stopping only inches from where she stood, forcing her to take a step back. The other man glanced curiously past her to the hedge.

"I'm trying to find my carriage," Jessie said calmly, showing him her best helpless smile. "Do you think you can help? It's a carriage from town. A spotted gelding."

"Yeah, I expect we could do that." He let his eyes trail hungrily over her bare shoulders, the soft shadow of her breasts. "Charlie, find the lady's carriage, you hear?" The second man grinned and walked off. His friend stepped back and watched Jessie. His mouth curled in a smile that plainly mirrored his thoughts. The two were dressed in reasonably fitting suits and new bowler hats. Still, the way they carried themselves said 'hired gun' to Jessie.

A carriage turned midway down the drive and made its way toward the house.

"Well, looks like Charlie done his job," the man told Jessie. "Headin' back to town, are you?"

"Yes. Thank you very much for your help."

"No trouble."

Jessie lifted her skirt to step aboard. The man touched her waist to give her a hand; his palm slid down her hips before Jessie could pull away. The driver flicked his reins and the horse trotted down the drive. Jessie could hear the men's muted laughter in the dark.

The man called Charlie had an ugly bruise on his jaw. Jessie wondered if he'd gotten it from Ki. Her heart still pounded from her encounter with the Indian. Lord, if he really had something from Platte! Somehow, she'd have to find him again. No—that didn't make sense. He knew who she was. It would be a lot safer to let him find her.

She leaned slightly forward in the seat and slipped her hands beneath her skirts, slid the derringer out of its holster on her thigh, and rested the weapon in her lap. The carriage was past the iron gate, back on the rutted road again. Marcus Hunter's face appeared in her head. Whatever he might be, she didn't think he was a man given easily to fear. Yet, when she'd mentioned Shelikhov, and Kodiak Burke's interest in the Russian...

What's going on here? Jessie wondered. What did Burke— and Hunter as well—want from Shelikhov? If he knew something, something that might be a danger to Burke's plans, why didn't Burke simply kill him, get him out of the way? Such drastic measures had never stopped him before.

Jessie jerked up straight as a dark figure suddenly appeared beside the carriage. She gripped the ivory-handled weapon and thumbed back the hammer. The figure moved in a blur, leaped aboard, and threw himself at the driver. Jessie fired, the flash from the blunt muzzle briefly lighting up the night. A hand gripped her throat and tossed her roughly on her back. She saw the man's eyes in the dark and wondered why the hell she hadn't guessed there'd be two instead of one.

Chapter 7

Thick fingers grasped her hair and jerked back her chin, exposing the long column of her throat. A desperate cry froze on her lips; she saw the glint of metal, the heavy blade inches from her flesh. Suddenly the man uttered a faint, peculiar sound; his eyes went wide with surprise. Jessie stared as he rose straight up in the air and disappeared.

"Jessie! Jessie, are you all right!"

"K–Ki?" Jessie blinked, saw his face close to her own, and threw her arms around his neck. "Oh God, am I ever glad to see you!"

"It's all right; it's over." He lifted her off the seat of the carriage and helped her to the ground. A man lay silent on the road, staring up at the sky.

"Ki, there was another one." She grasped his hand tightly. "I–I got off a shot."

"You hit him but you didn't stop him," Ki said. "He's gone. I didn't have time to go after him."

"The driver?"

"I don't know. Stay here." Ki left her and vanished around the back of the carriage. In a moment he was back. "Dead. The man you winged got him with a blade. There's a lot of blood. He probably took off back to Burke's."

Jessie let out a breath. "If he makes it, Burke will send enough men to finish the job." She looked at Ki and glanced at the rig. "I think we'd better vacate the premises, friend."

Ki shook his head. "Not in that." He took her hand and led her into the dark. Something moved and Jessie made out the ghostly shapes of two horses in the trees.

"They were just waiting here, waiting for me to pass." Jessie repressed a shudder. "Burke sent them on ahead and . . ." She paused and looked curiously at Ki. "And where were *you* all this time? Just taking a late night stroll, I suppose."

Ki looked pained. "You thought I'd let you wander out to Kodiak Burke's by yourself. Is that what you thought?"

"Well, yes. Maybe."

"I hitched a ride on the back of the carriage, Jessie. Got off at the gate and waited. When you came back out, I got on again."

Jessie bit her lip and looked at the ground. "I'm kinda glad you thought of that."

"You didn't leave me any choice," he said bluntly. "Going out there was a foolish idea. I told you that—you decided not to listen. Nothing new, but—"

"Okay, you were right. But the trip wasn't useless. I think I learned a couple things."

"Tell me later," said Ki. "I don't want to hang around here." He led the horses out on the road.

"Someone'll find the carriage," said Jessie, "and the driver and Burke's man. The fella at the stable knows who hired this thing."

"So what?" Ki said dully. "What difference does it make?"

"I keep forgetting," Jessie sighed. "No sheriff, no laws. Nobody cares."

"Except Burke."

"Uh-huh. Except Burke. Let's get going, okay?" Jessie lifted her long skirt up to her thighs and threw a slender leg over the

55

saddle. Riding horseback in an evening gown didn't seem to be a practical idea. The horse shied and danced away, and Jessie looked down and saw the still body in the road. It wasn't Charlie, or the man who'd helped her into the carriage. She'd never seen him before.

Ki guessed her thoughts. "It's one of Maksutova's crew; we've met." He turned his mount in a half circle and headed back toward the lights of Sitka, keeping off the road in the cover of the trees.

How long would it take the man she'd shot to reach Burke's? Jessie wondered. Ten, fifteen minutes? Not much longer. Which meant in a half hour at the outside the place would be crawling with Burke's riders. Jessie frowned in thought and ducked under a low-hanging branch. "Hunter," she decided, spitting out the name. Marcus Hunter *was* in Burke's pay and he'd gone straight to the man and told him—told him Jessie Starbuck knew something about the business with Shelikhov. She didn't, but Hunter couldn't know that for sure. Certainly Burke had plans to kill her when it suited his needs. Hunter's information had simply hurried him along. Jessie clenched her fists in anger, remembering Hunter's expression of concern.

Ki raised his hand and slowed his mount to a halt. Jessie rode up to his side. "There," Ki pointed. "I think that's the hotel—in that bunch of buildings down the slope."

"Looks like it," said Jessie. There was no sign of life in the town. A dog barked somewhere near St. Michael's. Jessie turned to Ki to speak; Ki's head jerked up and his eyes darted quickly to the right. She heard it, then, the sound of horses on the road, the squeak of saddle leather.

"Didn't take 'em much time," Ki muttered darkly. "Come on, get down—there's cover over there."

Jessie slid quickly off her horse and led it through heavy brush. There was a thick stand of western hemlock and yellow cedar on the slope. The road was less than twenty yards away, but no one would spot them unless they rode right into the grove. Ki handed his reins to Jessie and slipped silently down the rise. One of Burke's riders had carried a Winchester on his saddle and Jessie had retrieved it, quietly levering a shell in the chamber. She felt like a fool, hunkered down on the wet ground in her evening gown, a rifle across her knees.

The mounts skittered nervously as Ki reappeared out of shadow. "Fifteen, twenty riders. They went right to the hotel first."

"Great," said Jessie, "now what?"

Ki's dark eyes found hers. "I'm going down there," he said evenly. "I'll get what I can from the hotel—packs, coats, whatever I can get away with."

Jessie stared. "Ki, you can't! Not with Burke's men there!"

"It's the last thing they'd expect me to do."

"It's the last thing *I'd* expect you to do," she said shortly. "It's a stupid idea."

"We're going to have to ride out of here," he said. "I don't have the slightest idea where and neither do you. We don't even have a map. We'll have to get off Baranof Island as quick as we can. If they'll let us. And after that—what? There's nothing directly east but British Columbia. Thousands of miles of nothing. And *no* one to help. I don't see doing what we've got to do with no blankets or gear." He arched a brow in her direction. "And you dressed up for the Governor's Ball."

"I can manage," she said ruefully. "We'll find a miner's cabin or something. I won't have you going down there and maybe—Ki! Damn it all, will you listen to me!"

"I'll be back," he said softly, slipping past her into the brush. "Just sit tight."

"Ki!" She let out a breath and leaned back against a tree. "Sit tight," she muttered to herself. "Now where the hell would I go?"

He stood in the shadow of the abandoned building, watching the front door of the hotel. The fat man with the wide-brimmed hat sat on the steps and made a smoke. Since Ki had been watching, five of Burke's men had gone inside. Three had come out and left. The other two were still there. Unless, he reminded himself, they'd gone out the back. He could see no reason for that, but it was something he had to consider.

Ki slipped around the building to an alley, walked thirty

yards west, and sprinted across the street. A few moments later he was circling past a smelly pile of garbage at the rear of the hotel. The cook came out of the café next door, relieved himself against the fence, and went back inside. Ki searched the night once more and walked silently up the hotel's back steps, opened the screen door, and stepped inside. A kerosene lamp glowed at the end of a narrow hall. The lobby had to be just beyond the corner. The lobby, and a few steps past it, the stairs. Ki drew the slim *tanto* blade from under his belt and held it loosely in his hand. The lamp was too bright, but there was nothing he could do about that. He moved to the end of the hall and peered cautiously around the corner. The lobby was empty. The fat man was still sitting on the steps outside. Two men stood above him. One passed around a bottle. Were they the two men who'd stayed inside? Or two more who'd arrived since Ki had left the front?

Ki went to the floor and bellied his way to the stairs, stopped and looked up into the dark, and then mounted the steps quickly without a sound. Pausing at the top, he took a calming breath and brought all his senses to bear, straining for the slightest hint of movement, a sound that didn't belong. The hall was pitch black; the light from below died halfway up the stairs. There was something, something there—a slight odor on the air, a smell that wasn't right...

Ki bent his legs in a crouch and moved through the darkness. His fingers found a door and then another. The next one was his own. He passed it and went on to Jessie's. His hand touched the edge of her door. Past it was empty space. Ki jerked back his fingers. Jessie's door was wide open.

Suddenly, the hairs at the back of his neck began to tingle. The smell was stronger now and Ki knew exactly what it was. He slid inside the room and pressed his back against the wall. Holding the knife at his side, he poked his free hand in his pocket, brought out a match, and struck it on the molding of the door. The light flared, painting harsh shadows on the walls. In the quick moment of brightness he saw the overturned chairs, the bare slats of the bed, the mattress split open on the floor, Jessie's clothes and belongings scattered to every corner of the room. A foot from where he stood he saw an Indian, the body that belonged to the mingling smells of death and defecation. His shirt was torn away and his trousers were bunched up about his ankles. His arms and legs were bent at awkward angles. He was split wide open from his sternum to his crotch, his life spilling out on the floor. Ki had seen him once before. He had disappeared in an alley a few blocks from Natalia's house.

The match died. He found another, held his breath, and went to the man's side. Lighting his second match, he lifted the man's right leg and then his arm. Ki's skin crawled. It was just as he'd imagined. Before the Indian died, someone had broken nearly every bone in his body.

"Maksutova!" Ki let the name hiss through his teeth. He didn't have the slightest doubt that the giant was responsible for this horror. But why? What was the Indian doing here? Why was he dead in Jessie's room?

It had happened very quickly, Ki knew—moments after Burke's riders had reached the hotel. He had spotted them from the slope and gone back to tell Jessie what he planned. The Indian had been in Jessie's room at that moment. Burke's men had found him and given him to Maksutova.

Something cold touched the edge of Ki's mind. He could still be here, right here in the hotel. Maybe he never left!

Ki pushed the thought aside, forcing his mind back to reason. He lit another match, shading it with the cupped hand to keep the light from the window. Working quickly now, he gathered up the things Jessie would need and moved on to his own room. They'd been there, too, scattering his few belongings. He stuffed a few things in his pack, then bent to pry a board from the floor. The small leather sack was there; he hefted it in his palm and felt the weight of a half dozen *shuriken* throwing stars. Dropping the sack in his jacket pocket, he opened the window silently and studied the night. Stepping out to the overhanging roof, he dropped to the narrow alley between the hotel and the café. He had Jessie's belongings and his own in two bundles. Moving toward the back of the hotel, he hefted the loads more comfortably on his shoulders. The fat man in the wide-brimmed hat stepped from behind the fence at the

59

back of the café. He was eating half a blueberry pie and walked directly into Ki's path. He stopped short, staring in disbelief. Ki dropped one of his packs and hit the man once in the mouth. The fat man crumbled—Ki picked up his bundles and ran.

"Goddamn, it's him!" a voice bellowed. Two of Burke's men burst through the rear door of the café. Gunfire rattled through the dark, tossing up dirt at Ki's heels. He muttered a curse and ducked into an alley. Voices called out across the night. Three horsemen in the street galloped past the alley. Ki heard the pair from the café right behind him. Straight ahead, then, or back the way he'd come. The two on his heels were lousy shots, but amateurs get lucky now and then.

Ki searched the street. Four men ran for the hotel. The three riders were gone. Hefting his packs, Ki bent low and darted across the street for the stretch of abandoned buildings. He stopped, held his breath, and listened. A volley of gunfire erupted behind the hotel, but Burke's men were firing at shadows. Ki sprinted down a sidestreet, staying close to the empty, clapboard structures. The sound of horses came from his right and he moved back quickly to his left and headed north.

The dark spire of St. Michael's was straight ahead. Ki paused to get his bearings. The Sitka Trading Company and Shelikhov's store were past the cathedral. He had to go right and past the edge of town toward Jessie. The riders were cutting him off on two sides, forcing him back to the waterfront. They couldn't know where he was going—but they knew if they could drive him to the water he was dead.

Ki waited until he was certain that they'd see him and know he was making a run. Clutching his packs under each arm, he sprinted across the darkened street. A shout went up at once. Guns blazed in Ki's direction; lead splintered rotten wood and showered Ki with geysers of wet earth. Ki kept moving. He circled the building in a dead run, rounded the corner, and turned back toward the street. Burke's men were yelling and waving their torches, firing blindly in the direction he'd disappeared. Ki stepped into the street and joined the tail end of the pursuit. Keeping his head low, he cut quickly to his left and vanished into shadow. Less than two minutes had passed. He had crossed the street, circled a building, and crossed back again. Now, he was standing exactly where he'd started.

The gunmen were poking their torches into alleys, peering into darkened buildings. If they didn't find something soon, Ki knew they'd turn back and start looking where they'd been. He dropped his packs to the ground and picked up a handful of stones. He loosed half a dozen, arcing then high over the roofs across the street. The stones rattled against wood. One lucky shot found a window. Burke's men swarmed to the sources of the noise. The low, throaty roar of a shotgun thundered twice. Ki picked up his bundles and moved swiftly up the street heading north.

A rider came out of nowhere, rounding a corner fast and nearly spilling himself out of the saddle.

"Knew I saw something," he shouted, "and by God I did!"

The shadow broke from the alley, stumbled and fell, and rose again. The horseman laughed and leaned out of his saddle. In one swift motion, Ki drew the slim *tanto* blade from his belt and sent it flying. The rider went rigid, clawed straight up for empty air. He bounced once in the saddle and hit the ground. The horse lowered its head and kept going.

"Who's there?" Ki called out softly. "Come out, it's all right."

A strangled, unearthly wail came from the shadows. Ki went stiff. The cry raised the hackles on the back of his neck. The figure came out of darkness and threw itself in his arms.

"Natalia!" Ki gripped the girl's shoulders and held her back, staring in disbelief. "Good God, what are you doing out here!"

"He killed him," Natalia moaned, her face contorted with pain. "Uncle Nikolai's dead, Ki. M—Maksutova split him open with a knife!"

61

Chapter 8

The girl trembled uncontrollably in his arms, her eyes locked on a horror he couldn't see.

"It's all right, Natalia," Ki said gently. "Just hang on; it's all right." He guided her to the shadows and ran quickly back to the street. Grabbing Burke's gunman under the arms, he dragged the limp body into the alley, retrieved his *tanto* blade, and plunged it several times in clean earth. The other riders would find the horse any moment—when they did, they would tighten the noose around his neck, block him off from any chance of escape. Finding his two packs in the alley, he joined Natalia again. She hadn't moved from the spot where he'd left her. He hoisted the bundles to his shoulder, took the girl's hand, and moved hurriedly through the narrow streets. A few more blocks and then the protective cover of the trees, the dark forest sweeping down from the hill. He heard the riders behind him, saw the bright flicker of torches to his left. Natalia moaned softly beside him, gasping for breath through her tears. Ki kept going. He could see the hill now above the rooftops to his right. Shouts rose up behind him and he knew they'd found the horse. A few men fired their guns in anger. Ki squeezed the girl's wrist and forced her to quicken her pace. Let the men do what they wanted. He would make it to the safety of the trees. Their anger alone couldn't kill him.

Jessie heard a sound, a branch snapping back against leather. Sighting down the barrel of a rifle she saw two shadows break into the clearing, saw the smaller figure sink to the ground.

"Jessie—easy, it's me."

"Ki!" With a quick sigh of relief she ran to him, held him a brief moment, then bent to the sobbing girl. Natalia's face was pale, her eyes glazed with shock and fear.

"Her uncle," Ki said at Jessie's shoulder, "they killed him. Maksutova."

"Oh, my God, no!" Jessie took the girl in her arms. "Natalia, I'm sorry."

"I am all right. I have to be all right." Natalia sat up and took a deep breath. She squeezed Jessie's hand and stared into the night. "I will kill him," she said without expression. "I swear by my uncle's name Maksutova will die at my hands." Her eyes blurred once again; she forced back the tears and looked at Jessie. "I am sorry. I will not weep for him again."

"You've got all the right in the world," Jessie told her. "You do what you have to do."

Ki returned from the edge of the clearing. "There are clothes in that pack," he told Jessie. "Change as fast as you can. We can't stay around here."

"I can't believe you went back to that hotel."

"There are a lot of things around this place I don't believe. Come on, let's make tracks."

Jessie changed quickly, shedding the thin evening gown and stuffing it under the root of a tree. In a moment she was clothed in worn denims, a cotton shirt, and boots. The night was cool and the fleece-lined leather jacket felt good about her shoulders. There was an extra pair of denims in the pack and Natalia slipped them on, leaving her cotton dress behind. Ki contributed

63

an oversize flannel shirt. Natalia protested, but he draped his own jacket around her. The sound of riders came to them from the road just below. Ki led the two horses from the trees.

"We can't go toward town," he said soberly. "South, maybe. There doesn't seem to be much there but rugged country."

"No, not south." Natalia firmly shook her head. "South will take us nowhere but to the end of Baranof Island and the ocean. We could get to Kupreanof from there, but there is too much open sea." She scraped a patch of dirt with her hands. "Look— Baranof is here; it is maybe a hundred miles long, twenty or twenty-five wide. It is eighty miles east to the mainland. Over other islands and water. We must go north. Here." She made a short loop above Sitka. "Chichagof Island is maybe twenty or so miles from where we are. It is no more than two or three miles across the channel. If we get there I think we can lose them. There is too much coast for them to watch."

Ki thought. "We have a few hours of dark left. If we ride up there and get over before morning . . ." He looked at Natalia. "We'll have to get our hands on some kind of boat. Will that be a problem?"

Natalia's voice was dead calm. "I will get us a boat. Do not concern yourself."

"And when we get to this other island," Jessie said, "what's the chance of getting help, maybe working our way back to the mainland?"

"I think you know the answer," Natalia said grimly. "There will be no help, Jessie. One does not depend on others in Alaska. Anyone we meet in the wilderness will belong to Burke. There are Indians, of course. But we cannot depend on them for much."

"Yeah, I guess I knew before I asked," Jessie sighed.

"All right," said Ki, "let's go. We need all the night we can get."

"Go north for a while," Natalia said, swinging up behind Ki, "then east. I know this island better than they do," she added bitterly. "It is my home, not theirs."

"There," she pointed, "there's the sea, and Chichagof Island beyond."

In the light of the stars, Jessie could make out a pale ribbon of water, a vague, dark mass of land against the night. Even in the middle of Alaska's summer, the gray stretch of water looked cold and forbidding. "Does anyone live there?" she asked the girl.

"Hoonahs. They speak the Tlingit tongue." Natalia started for the path down to the shore. Ki stopped her.

"I want to take a look down there," he said. "If this is our best way off the island, Burke's men are going to know that, too. They'll be around somewhere."

Natalia shook him off. "There are hundreds of little hidden bays and inlets on this coast. An old fisherman has a house down there. His name is Andrei Tchitchinoff. He is—he was a friend of my uncle's. It is his boat we will use."

"Will anyone else know about him?" asked Jessie.

"Who can say?" Natalia shrugged. "Maksutova could have heard of him in Sitka but I doubt it. No one in the Russian community will speak to that man. They know he belongs to Burke." She turned her eyes up to Ki. "There is no time for you to go down there alone. I have never tried to find Tchitchinoff's place in the dark. If you go down, then come back looking for us . . ."

"She's right," said Jessie. "We'd better stick together."

"It's your island," Ki told the girl, "lead on."

"We will have to leave the horses. They are useless to us now."

Ki nodded. He quickly removed the saddles and blankets and bridles and slapped the mounts away. Watching them vanish up the valley, he felt as if they were closing a door behind them. There was no way to turn back now, no place to go except the sea.

The small cedar cabin was nearly hidden in the trees, its timbered walls covered with vines and second growth. Jessie was sure most anyone would miss the place in broad daylight. It seemed as if Natalia had been gone forever when she suddenly appeared again.

"It is all right," she whispered. "The boat is down past the trees. Not far." She hefted a heavy brown bag in her hands.

65

"Food," she explained. "Dried salmon and black bread. I told him I would leave the boat on the other side."

Ki raised a brow. "And he'll find it?"

"Oh, yes. Of course." She raised her chin in defiance. "He is a Russian fisherman. The boat belongs to him. It will tell him where it is."

The conviction in her voice told him she had no doubt at all this was true.

Natalia walked ahead. Jessie heard the sound of water against the rocky shore. The boat was beached on a gravel bank under the trees. In the half light, its hull looked like the gray flanks of some bloated fish. Ki turned it over and dragged it to the water as quietly as he could. Natalia retrieved the oars.

"I hope you know how to row," she told him. "The current between the islands can be very tricky."

"I've done it," Ki said evenly. "It's not my favorite sport."

He guided the boat out of the sheltered bay, staying close to the trees that lined the shore. Open water would be the danger; even in the dark someone watching from the heights above could spot the boat. He wanted to get around the headland to his left where he could see in both directions. The sea would open up and give him a clear view of the shore.

"Ki, over there—look!" Jessie's harsh words turned him around. A light bobbed in the water not fifty yards away. Ki frantically moved the boat in an awkward circle and put his shoulders to the oars. He fought the swift water that threatened to pull him out to sea. Finally, the oars took command, bringing the craft back into the safety of their own side of the headland.

"Great," Ki said harshly, "it didn't take 'em long. Did either of you get a good look at it?"

"It's a small steamer," said Jessie. "I saw it against the sky."

"I know this ship," Natalia said shakily. "It is Burke's and it is very fast. They must have brought it up at once through Sitka Sound past Kruzov Island. And Ki, I–I think I saw riders as well. On the shore. I'm almost certain."

Ki cursed under his breath. "They'll use the riders to flush us out. If we make for the strait they've got the steamer to run us down. Hell, if they can keep us bottled up until morning they'll have us cold."

"We'll have to get back to shore and run for it," said Jessie. "There's nothing else to do."

"I can't outrow 'em," Ki said grimly. He bent to the oars, thinking about the horses running free on shore.

"Ki—" Jessie's hand tightened on his arm. "There it is; it's coming!"

"Over there," Natalia pointed, "straight ahead, Ki."

"There's nothing there but rock," Ki protested. "It's twenty feet high."

"Ki, please—do as I say. Quickly!"

Ki let out a breath and aimed the bow of the boat for the sheer stone wall. He could feel Natalia's hand pressed hard against his shoulder as she stared intently at the shore. The sound of the steamer grew louder in his ears.

"Left," Natalia urged, *"left*, Ki."

Ki did as he was told, wondering if the girl had lost her mind. The rocky wall was out of shadow. The men on the steamer would spot the dark shape of the boat against the lighter gray of the stone.

"There, there!" Natalia exclaimed. Her fingers dug into his shoulder.

"There what? I don't—" He saw it then, a narrow cleft in the solid wall, a line of darkness hardly wider than their boat. He made for the spot at once, shipping the oars and reaching out to keep the sides of the boat from scraping. Suddenly, the boat was plunged into solid darkness. Ki heard the hollow sound of water lapping stone. He could feel the damp surface only inches from his head.

"I was here when I was a child," Natalia whispered. "Andrei Tchitchinoff took me fishing in this very boat many times. I was very frightened. He told me this place was where the ghosts of seals went to live."

"I think he was right," said Jessie. "Ki, back here I'm only a couple of feet from the entrance. I can hear the engine. It's not coming any closer."

"They will not find us," Natalia said with a confidence Ki didn't share. "Even in bright sunlight you can pass this place and notice nothing."

"Maybe," said Ki. "I'm not real anxious to find out. Jessie, when that steamer gets out of sight again I want to try it." He waited, sitting quietly in the dark, straining for the noise of the ship, the sound of Burke's riders along the shore. Even when the steamer was gone they wouldn't be sure of the riders. They'd have to take their chances. There was no other choice. They might lose themselves in the dark on the island but the dark wouldn't last forever.

"Natalia," he said carefully, "maybe you don't want to talk about it, but everything happened so fast back there in town—"

"You are right," she said stiffly, "I do not want to talk about it, Ki. Please."

"Don't blame you. I'm sorry. But I think it's something Jessie and I have to know. Your uncle—you said Maksutova killed him, but you didn't say why. Why did he do it, Natalia?"

"I cannot talk about this. Don't you understand? I can still see it—what that monster did to Nikolai!"

"Your uncle knew something, didn't he?"

"Why–why do you ask that?"

Jessie heard the alarm in the girl's voice. "Please. I know this is hard for you. Trust us, won't you? Kodiak Burke wanted something from your uncle. What was it?"

"A–a stupid story," Natalia said bitterly. "A stupid story that isn't even true."

"Burke thought it was worth killing over," Jessie said plainly. "What was this story about, Natalia?"

Natalia sighed in the dark. "My grandfather left Sitka to sail back to Russia. It was all a big secret of some kind. He told my grandmother that when he returned they would be very rich. My father and my uncle were very small. Ten or twelve, I think. The ship was lost at sea. They never saw my grandfather again."

"And what was supposed to be on this ship?" Ki asked.

Natalia hesitated a long moment. "Gold. The ship was the *Okhotsk* and it was supposed to be full of gold. This is what my grandmother told my father and my uncle when they were older. Ki, it is only a story, a tale for children. God, it happened over forty years ago!"

"A story with no truth to it at all," Jessie said thoughtfully. "And Kodiak Burke hounded your uncle for it and finally killed him."

"Yes, yes that is what happened."

"I don't think I believe that," Jessie said evenly. "I don't think you do, either."

"Believe what you like," Natalia said harshly, "it is true!"

Ki leaned past the girl and spoke to Jessie. "There's something I haven't had a chance to tell you. I think I'd better get it out now because I think Natalia ought to hear it, too. Jessie, I found a dead Indian in your hotel room—killed the very same way as Nikolai—both split open by a knife.

"My God!" Jessie gasped. "Ki, there was an Indian at Burke's house. A servant. He tried to talk to me. Burke's men came up and he disappeared. He said he had something for me from Platte."

"I think I saw the same man on the street," Ki said grimly. "He looked at me and ran. Hell, I didn't think much about it."

"Burke's house!" Natalia's words exploded in the darkness. "What were you doing up there? You went to see him? You are full of questions for me, now I will ask you!"

"Natalia . . ."

"I remember. You had on the pretty party dress back there in the trees. You—you go to this bastard's party while his man is murdering my uncle!"

"Natalia, just shut up a minute, all right?" Ki said harshly.

"Friends, ha! How can I believe what you tell me?"

"You might start with the fact that we're here," Ki said soberly, "trying to keep Burke from slitting your throat."

"Maybe," Natalia muttered, "still . . ."

"We can talk about it later," Ki told her. "There's no time for it now. Jessie, I'm going to push us toward the entrance with my hands. You do the same back there and make sure we don't bump the walls."

"Right." Jessie leaned back in the stern as far as she could, hands pressed against the rock above her head. After the darkness of the fissure, the night outside seemed unnaturally bright. They brought the boat out through the hole without a sound.

Ki swept his eyes in every direction, watching, listening, every sense alert. Finally, he lowered the oars carefully into the water, rowing with slow, even strokes.

When they passed the headland again, the current caught the bow and swept them rapidly toward the east. This time, Ki made no attempt to fight it. The current added to his speed, taking him quickly away from the shore. When they were well out of sight he would change his course and row northwest for Chichagof Island. He looked over his shoulder, studying the dark mass of land across the strait. He stared right at the steamer, unaware of what he was seeing from one beat of his heart to the next.

A quick cry of alarm died in Natalia's throat, and the steamer suddenly detached itself from darkness, appeared out of shadow against the peaks of Chichagof Island. A shout went up across the water; a split second later the white flash from the muzzle of a rifle brightened the night.

Chapter 9

"Get down," Ki yelled. "Keep low!"

Natalia groaned and hugged the bottom of the boat. Jessie went flat, twisted on her back, and levered a shell into the Winchester.

"No, wait," Ki told her, "don't draw their fire." He put all the strength he could muster into his arms, driving the small craft into the darkness. Lead whined dangerously close to his head. He could see shots dimpling the water on either side. The sound he dreaded hearing reached his ears as the steamer's powerful engines roared into life. It wouldn't take them long, he knew. Four minutes, five at the most. The steamer would reach them and that would be that. They would take the women alive, carry them back to Burke. Jessie was deadly with the rifle and she'd make them pay right up to the end. He risked a look over his shoulder. The small steamer was picking up speed. Now, the boat was ablaze with light; lanterns swung from the sides, bobbed above the water forward and aft. Gunmen held torches over the bow. One man tossed a burning brand into the air. For an instant, the rowboat was bathed in harsh light. Gunfire rattled through the night and the men laughed.

"Jessie, Natalia," Ki yelled, "jump and try to make it back to shore. It's better than staying here!"

"I can't swim," Natalia said angrily.

"I can't either," said Jessie.

"Like hell you can't—you can swim like an eel! Give me that rifle and get out of here, Jessie!"

Jessie didn't answer. Instead, she came up on her knees, steadied the Winchester, and calmly squeezed off half a dozen shots at the steamer. Glass shattered. A man gave a hoarse cry of alarm. A harsh roll of thunder reached Ki's ears. A lantern exploded, lighting up the water and sending a long tongue of flame into the air. A gunman shrieked and tumbled into the water. Ki stared as a fist-sized hole appeared in the side of the bridge. He blinked at Jessie and saw she wasn't firing at all. She jabbed one arm to her left and Ki saw a burst of yellow flame from the end of the headland. Sound rolled across the water once more. A square foot of decking exploded, sending a shower of wooden splinters over the gunmen in the bow. Fire from the broken lantern licked at the bridge. The weapon on shore roared again. In the light of sudden flames Ki saw a man's head disappear. The steamer wheeled crazily to port and turned out to sea. Ki and the two women were forgotten as the men aboard the steamer turned their weapons to the shore. The man on the end of the spit fired again, wrecking havoc aboard the ship.

"That son of bitch has a Sharps," Ki grinned, pounding one fist into the other. "Look at him!"

"They're running," Natalia said in awe. "They're leaving, Ki!"

The man on shore methodically fired one round after another, loading and reloading the heavy rifle as if he were dropping buffalo from a stand. Someone found the wheel of the steamer and brought it to bear, heading rapidly to the west. The wind blew a heavy pall of smoke from the shooter's post. Ki saw the man lift the Sharps off of a Y-shaped shooting stick and wave the weapon over his head.

"Come on, damn it," he shouted, "get me out of here. That shooting's going to bring back the riders!"

Jessie's face went slack. "Ki, I know that voice! No, uh-uh, it can't be."

Ki rowed quickly toward the spit, fighting the strong current of the strait. The man glanced anxiously over his shoulder, hoisted the rifle over his head, and walked out in the water to the boat.

"Evening, Miss Starbuck," he said calmly, "Natalia. And I guess you're Ki."

"Hunter!" Jessie stared as Ki helped the man into the boat. "What are *you* doing here!"

Hunter raised a curious brow. "You mean I went to all that trouble and you didn't even notice?"

"He is a spy, that's what he is," Natalia said tightly. Her eyes flashed at the tall man. "He is a friend of Kodiak Burke!"

"If he is, he's got a funny way of showing it," said Ki. "He just saved your neck, lady."

Natalia made a noise and turned away.

"I think I owe you an apology, mister," said Jessie.

"None needed." Hunter touched his hat. "I didn't give you much reason to show trust." He glanced at Ki and nodded. "I'll spell you on those oars if you want. We're going to have company in a minute. I'd just as soon be out of range when we do."

"I could use a little rest," Ki said soberly. "Thank you." He moved back to sit with Natalia while Hunter took his place. Ki saw at once the man had done some rowing before.

"I'll answer your question, Miss Starbuck," Hunter said, "and save you the trouble of asking. Natalia's right. I've been hanging in pretty close to Burke for a couple months. I had a good reason. You'll have to take my word for that."

"I've still got questions," Jessie told him, "but I can wait for answers."

"You showed up at the right spot at the right time, friend," Ki said curiously. "That was a very neat trick."

Hunter grinned. He knew what Ki was really asking. "You've

got a polite way of puttin' it, I'll give that to you. Burke trusts me, Ki—at least he did. Don't imagine he does now. I was standing right with him when word came back you folks had shot up one of his men on the road. He sent a bunch of riders into town and some others up to this end of the island to cut you off. Along with that steamer of his. I don't like the man but he's a smart bastard. He knew you'd have to get off of Baranof if he didn't catch you in town. I followed the riders and watched the boat till it found you." Hunter's features went sober and he looked directly at Natalia. "I didn't know he planned on going after your uncle. If I had, I would have stopped him. That's the truth."

Natalia bit her lip and turned away.

"Natalia," Jessie said solemnly, "I'm sorry but I think I'm partly responsible for Nikolai's death. I asked Mr. Hunter at that party why he and Burke were so interested in your uncle. He tried to warn me off. He knew that was a dangerous question and I didn't. Not then."

"Burke knew you and Ki had been talking to Shelikhov," said Hunter. "He didn't know why but he's a pretty careful man. He'd been pushing Shelikhov hard—trying to scare him into telling him what he wanted to know. When you took off, Miss Starbuck, I guess he decided not to take any chances. He didn't know what Shelikhov had told you but he couldn't afford to leave any loose ends. If you happened to get away somehow, and Shelikhov had said something to you . . ."

"You're saying I forced his hand and got Nikolai killed," Jessie said grimly. "I'm afraid that's true, Mr. Hunter."

"Don't blame yourself. It would have happened. It just happened a little sooner."

"*Nothing* would have happened if everyone had left us alone!" Natalia said fiercely. Tears of anger blurred her eyes. "I watched him die—they made me watch what Maksutova did to him!" She pounded her fists on her knees. "My uncle couldn't tell them anything because there is nothing to tell about that foolish legend!"

Marcus Hunter looked at her. "Natalia," he said gently, "Kodiak Burke knows about the Aleut. He knows your uncle talked to him."

The girl's eyes went wide. She stared in horror at Hunter. "No. No, he does not. He—he couldn't!"

Jessie frowned curiously at Hunter, then at Natalia. In a moment, Hunter stopped rowing and rested his arms. The boat bobbed slightly in the gentle swell. Hunter stared out across the water.

"There's more to this story than Natalia wants to tell—more than she knows, too. Three months ago, an Aleut came into Sitka from the north country. An old man, seventy or more. He went to Nikolai Shelikhov and told him the *Okhotsk* didn't sink on the way back to Russia. He said a storm tossed the ship up on the ice. He was one of the crewmen. Natalia's grandfather and everyone else on board died. The Aleut was the only survivor. The ship is still there."

"Is this true, Natalia?" asked Jessie. "Is it?"

"It—it's true," Natalia said tightly. "There was an Indian and he came to my uncle." She glared at Marcus Hunter. "How could you know this? My uncle told no one. No one except me!"

"He shouldn't have, Natalia, but he did," said Hunter. "He—I'm sorry, he got drunk one night with an old friend and did some bragging. He told this friend he wasn't always going to be a storekeeper. That soon he was going to be rich. The friend goaded him on and got the story out of him. I'm afraid your uncle trusted the wrong man, one who's been on Burke's payroll for a long time, keeping an eye on the Russian community. He went right to his boss with the story."

"Who," Natalia demanded, "who is this man!"

"Podushkin. Stephen Podushkin."

"Podushkin!" Natalia paled in disbelief.

"You mind if I ask just how you came to know all this?" said Ki.

"His good friend Burke told him," Natalia snapped. "How do you think?"

Hunter let out a breath. "I found out the same way I learned a lot of things. I kept my eyes and ears open. I flattered Kodiak Burke and told him he was the smartest man I ever met. He figured I could be useful and let me stay around." Hunter paused a moment. "Whenever Burke wanted to do some serious talking he'd walk a man out behind his house. Away from the servants and everyone else inside. I followed him a couple of times; once I overheard him talking to Maksutova about what Podushkin had told him. Burke wanted Maksutova to track down the Aleut but the old Indian had already disappeared."

Natalia looked at Hunter but said nothing. Jessie sighed and swept her hair over her shoulders. "And Kodiak Burke believes this story? That's what I find kinda hard to swallow. He's not the sort of man to go chasing after lost treasure ships. At least *I* don't see him that way."

"You're right, he's not," said Hunter. "Kodiak Burke wouldn't waste a minute running after some half-baked dream. Unless he figured there was a lot more to it than that." He paused and let his eyes flick briefly to Natalia. "When the Aleut told his story about the storm, and Podushkin brought the tale to Burke, Burke was curious enough to check it out. The same thought occurred to me so I knew right off what he was up to. I let him do all the snooping, and when he found what he wanted I knew right where to look."

"And where was that?" asked Jessie.

"Old shipping records from the days when this was Russian territory. He found when the *Okhotsk* sailed out of Sitka Sound over forty years ago. The exact time of day they weighed anchor. Finding the next piece of the puzzle was a little harder, but Burke managed and so did I. A big storm blew up in the Pacific the day after the *Okhotsk* sailed. It tore up the coast for a week."

"So Burke knew the old Indian wasn't lying." Jessie sucked in a breath. "There was a storm, and it could have wrecked the ship before it got out to sea."

"That's it. The Aleut wouldn't just happen to get lucky—make up a story about a ship in a storm and it turns out there *was* such a storm."

"There's something else here, too." Jessie reached out and grasped Natalia's hands in her own. The girl tried to pull away, but Jessie refused to let her go. "Natalia, look at me. Please. After what's happened to you I don't blame you for the way you feel. Trust me. Will you do that?"

76

"I like you, Miss Starbuck." Natalia looked into the darkness. "I do not think you and Ki would betray me. This man, though . . ."

"I don't think he'd be here if he wasn't with us, Natalia. Now tell me, did the Aleut tell your uncle where to find this ship? He did, didn't he?"

"No, never!" Again, she tried to pull away. "He knew nothing. I told you, there is nothing to tell!"

"I don't think that's true. I'm sorry. Maksutova wouldn't have killed him before he found out what Burke wanted to know. Once your uncle was dead, Burke would have lost his source of information. The Aleut had disappeared. I don't think Nikolai would have told you because he wouldn't want you to have such dangerous information. If Maksutova killed him, it was because he was satisfied he'd gotten what he wanted. That's how it happened, isn't it? Maksutova killed him, you managed to get away, and—"

"God, please—stop it!" Natalia jerked away and sobbed into her hands. Her shoulders trembled and Ki reached out to touch her. His eyes met Jessie's and it was easy to guess her thoughts. It was true, then—there was a whole shipload of gold lost somewhere on the frozen coastline of Alaska. With wealth like that in his hands, Kodiak Burke could wield unbelievable power—for himself and his Prussian masters as well. The cartel would own Alaska—lock, stock, and barrel. The riches from this vast land would give them a giant step toward their ultimate goal: economic and political control of the United States.

"Natalia," he said, "what Jessie told you is true. Trust us, please. If you keep this secret to yourself, Burke will win. It means Nikolai died for nothing. He'll take what rightfully belongs to the Shelikhovs, to you."

"Ki, I don't *want* that damned treasure," Natalia moaned. "I don't want it!"

"Do you want him to have it? Do you want him to take it without even a—"

"All right!" Natalia pulled away. Her voice trembled as she spoke. *"Yakutat."* The word seemed to stick in her throat. "That is all that my uncle said before he was murdered. He said it over and over and begged Maksutova to stop his torture. Yakutat. He died speaking this word!"

"My God, of course." Marcus Hunter let out a breath. The oars went still in his hands. "Yakutat Bay. It *has* to be." He looked straight at Jessie, his eyes dark and intent. "Yakutat Bay is north of here on the coast. And the ice—the ship in the ice. The biggest damn glacier in Alaska is right there. Malaspina! Christ, yes, Yakutat Bay!"

"You said north. How far north?" asked Ki.

"Uh—250 miles, something like that." Hunter bit his lip in thought. "It makes sense—all the sense in the world. There was a settlement there. Slavorossiya. And it was the Shelikhov family's company that built the place. Seventeen-nineties. Ninety-five, I think. If there was a storm, Natalia's grandfather would try to find shelter for the ship. And he'd sure as hell know about Yakutat Bay."

"If you're right," Jessie said darkly, "Kodiak Burke will head for that place as soon as it's light—if he isn't on his way right now."

"You can bet on it."

"How long will it take him to get there?"

"Couple days or more—depends on how big a hurry he's in. His steamer's not that large, and he'll have another vessel trailing along with the men and supplies he'll need." Hunter forced a grin. "If Yakutat Bay is all he knows, he's got a hell of a search on his hands. I've seen charts of the place. The Malaspina Glacier is maybe 1500 square miles of ice. The ice sheet's fifty miles long—slides right down the flanks of Mount St. Elias."

"The *Okhotsk* isn't sitting somewhere in plain sight," Ki mused. "Someone would have spotted it before now. If the place is as big as you say it is, you're right. Burke's got his work cut out for him."

"Unless he knows more than just Yakutat Bay." Hunter glanced meaningfully at Natalia. "That's all, isn't there? He doesn't know more than that, does he?"

"No," Natalia said tightly. She refused to look at Hunter.

78

"That's all. I *told* you that was all."

Ki wanted to believe her—but he wished he could see her eyes when she spoke.

Jessie stood on a low ridge in the shadow of a thick grove of tall, blue-green spruce.

"They'll come," said Hunter, guessing her thoughts. "Burke will go after that gold, but he won't forget us. There'll be a boatload over today sometime. They'll talk to the Indians and give them some money and they'll tell them right where we went." Burke made a noise in his throat. "Pretty good day of business for the Hoonahs. Only horses on the island worse than the ones we bought are the nags Burke's men are goin' to get."

Jessie knew he was watching her, studying her from the corner of his eye while she looked out over the strait. When she turned to face him, he met her gaze and held it. "You didn't even blink when I said I was going on north—that I had to stop Burke if I could. A man with any sense would know that's a damn fool idea. But you didn't say a thing, Mr. Hunter. I wonder why that is?"

Hunter shrugged. "Maybe I don't have any sense, either."

Jessie shook her head. "You'd already decided to go yourself. It had nothing to do with me. Don't tell me any different." Hunter didn't answer. "What is it," Jessie went on, "the gold? Or something else?"

"I've got reasons. I told you that before. Might be they're as good as the ones you're not sharing, Miss Starbuck."

"That might be," said Jessie. The sun appeared abruptly over the mountains, turning the gray water to molten iron.

★

Chapter 10

"We have to try to stop him," said Jessie. "It's either that or let him do whatever he wants. And don't tell me it's a crazy idea. Please."

"Why should I?" Ki said soberly. "I'm sure you already know it."

"As long as we have to run, we might as well run in the right direction. Burke might not expect us to do that."

Ki didn't answer. Jessie urged her mount over the rocky trail, ducking to avoid a low branch. Marcus Hunter rode ahead. She could see his tall form in the saddle; he vanished and reappeared through slim columns of dark Sitka spruce. Natalia rode behind, off to herself. She had said very little about the decision to go north after Burke. There was pain in her eyes, anger, and resignation.

For an instant, the thick forest opened on a clearing, revealing an unbelievably bright blue sky. Jessie turned in the saddle and looked to the south. From the glacial-carved ridge she could see the somber mountains of Baranof Island across the strait.

An hour later Marcus Hunter called a halt. They stopped as long as they dared to rest the horses and eat. Natalia shared her dried salmon and black bread. Hunter had bargained with the Hoonah Indians for some kind of deer meat. When he cut into the rock-hard slab they found it was too putrid to eat. Hunter angrily tossed the meat far down the ridge. Score one for the Indians, thought Jessie.

The Hoonahs had sensed the whites needed help and had little room to bargain. Hunter had to take the worn-out horses or nothing at all. Jessie remembered the slack, unsmiling faces, the brooding caution mixed with a hatred carved as deep into their features as the years.

Hunter drew a rough map on a scrap of paper. "We'll have to cross water again when we get to the end of Chichagof Island," he told them. "It's a bigger stretch of water than we made last night—twenty miles, maybe. We could cross over east before that—head for the mainland across the islands, or work up along the Chilkat Range and cut back northwest toward Yakutat Bay." He looked in turn at Jessie, Ki, and Natalia. "This is a pretty big island and the country's wild and rugged. What I'm saying is, there are several different things we can do, different ways to go. Burke's men are coming after us, but Burke won't spare too many hands from his trip to Yakutat Bay. Unless the Hoonahs help them track us, I don't think we're in much danger if we keep moving."

"The Hoonahs will help," Natalia said flatly. "If Burke's men offer them money or goods they will take it. They will at least pretend to track us, but I don't think they will put out any effort to find us. They have no reason to like us or hate us more than they do Burke's men. We are all whites."

"You've got a good point," Hunter agreed. "Unless they're smart enough to offer a big reward to the Indians if we're caught. I don't think we can rule that out."

Jessie squinted at Hunter's map. "So we've got all these different ways to go. Which do you figure is the best? Natalia, you live up here. Any ideas?"

Natalia shook her head. "He's right," she said darkly, "the country is very wild. I don't think it matters."

"I think we ought to keep going a few miles and then cut

down to the eastern coast of the island," said Hunter. "At least it'll be easier riding. And faster."

"They might figure that too," Ki suggested.

"They might," Jessie sighed. "We can't outguess them, but they don't know what we're thinking either. I suppose it comes out even. I think there's merit in getting down off these rocky ridges. It's pretty slow going—and if we try to take the country any faster we're going to lose a horse. That wouldn't be a good idea."

Hunter pushed back his Stetson. "Running for your life's got advantages and disadvantages in Alaska," he said dryly. "The good part is it's big and there are plenty of places to hide. The bad part is you're on your own. You're not goin' to find any help. No law, no army, no telegraph—no nothing." He faced them all again. "If anyone's got an idea they think's better I'm sure willing to listen. I know roughly where we are and that's about all."

Ki shook his head. "The coast sounds fine. There are too many choices to make. We won't know if we're right until it's done."

"Maybe that's a big advantage for our side," said Jessie. "If it is, we can sure use it."

They came down out of the high country late in the afternoon, keeping to the trees that trailed nearly to the water. There were hundreds of narrow bays and inlets. And across the water, more misty islands; more dark, forested peaks.

"Fish again," said Jessie, "just what I wanted."

"There was a café down the way a piece," Hunter said absently. "They had some thick beefsteaks and fried potatoes and hot coffee, but I figured you folks were all settled in."

"You could have gone all night without talking about steaks," Jessie told him.

"Wishing you were back in Texas about now?"

Jessie turned and nodded as Hunter sat down beside her. "Some, I guess. This is great country, but I can think of better ways to see it." She glanced back and saw Natalia curled up in shadow under a blanket past the fire. The first stars appeared over the far mountains. Night birds swooped low over the water. A big fish broke water near by.

"Where's Ki? You've seen him?"

"He's out scouting around. Back up on the ridge where we left the trail. Wanted to sniff things out. When he gets back I'm taking the first watch. He'll spell me about midnight or one. We don't figure Burke's men will come up on us in the dark in this kind of country but you can't ever tell."

"I guess." Jessie was silent a long moment. "You think that story's true, don't you, Mr. Hunter? A ship up there in the ice full of gold."

"You think maybe we could drop the mister and the miss? I'd say it's time enough now."

Jessie grinned. "I don't know. We haven't been properly introduced. What is it, Marcus or Mark?"

"Mark's fine, unless you're my mother. Then it's 'Marcus Joseph Hunter, come here this minute'—still."

"She's living, then?"

"Uh-huh. Dad's not but she is. Running the farm with my younger brother's help."

"And where might that be?"

"Virginia. The Hunters have been there forever. Farmers and planters—wearin' out the land." He hurried over the words; Jessie could see he was anxious to turn the conversation away from himself. She was more than a little curious, but decided not to push.

"And yes," he went on, "I believe the ship's there. I think the old Aleut was telling the truth. Why the hell he suddenly decided to come down south and tell his story after all these years I couldn't say. Indians will do things like that some-times—get a notion."

"Ki got a little out of Natalia this afternoon. Not much. The Indian wanted money from Nikolai. Nikolai gave him a little, but the Aleut wasn't happy with what he got."

Hunter shrugged. "I figured it was something like that."

"And you still believe him. The Indian, I mean. I know there's the business about the storm hitting at just the right time. It does lend truth to the story. It just seems fanciful to

83

me, Mark. I can't help it. Treasure ships full of gold, frozen in the ice. It's like all the pirate stories you hear along the Texas coast."

"I know. It's the classic buried treasure tale. But you'll notice Kodiak Burke believes it, too."

"And the storm, it could have lifted up that ship and hurled it on the glacier? Is that possible?"

"You ever been in a real Pacific storm?"

Once more, Jessie recalled her father's tales of the *tai-fung*. "No. No, I haven't. But I think I know what they can do."

Jessie stared into the night. An ember popped like a bullet behind her. "There's something you ought to know," she began. "I haven't told you because there's been no time. When I was leaving Burke's place last night—Lord, was that just last night? Anyway, an Indian approached me. He worked in Burke's house. I saw him in there earlier. He said he had something for me from Hiram Platte. Burke's men came out just then and he disappeared. Ki found him later. In my hotel room. Split open just like Natalia's uncle."

"Jesus Christ!" Hunter let out a breath and stared. "Maksutova again."

"Yes. Maksutova. Mark, did you ever overhear Burke say anything about Platte? About—about what Platte might have known about Burke's operation?"

"No." Hunter shook his head. "Nothing. I was lucky to learn as much as I did, Jessie. Burke's a careful man."

"But you know he was responsible for Hiram Platte's death."

Hunter forced a bitter laugh. "Hell, I didn't have to eavesdrop to learn that—everyone in Sitka knows Platte stood up to Burke more than once. And they also know the Tlingits had great respect for Platte. Using an Indian knife to kill him was Burke's idea of a little joke."

Jessie frowned. "I keep wondering what Hiram Platte told that Indian to give me. It had to do with Burke, of course. Burke knew—or suspected—that Platte had put something on paper. Something pretty damaging about what Burke was up to in Alaska. He tore up Platte's place looking for it. Lord, Mark, that Indian died because he was loyal to Platte. He risked trying to reach me to keep a dead man's wish!"

"Jessie . . ." Hunter reached out and grasped her hand. Jessie didn't protest. It was comforting to feel his touch and she was glad to have him near. She couldn't hold Mark's secrets against him, his reasons for getting close to Kodiak Burke, to pursue him now into the north. It was more than a ship full of gold; she was somehow certain of that. If he wanted to tell her, then he would. She had secrets of her own she wasn't ready to share with him.

They sat for a long moment without speaking. She could feel his eyes upon her and knew he wasn't thinking about Burke or what might lay ahead. She rested her head on his shoulder, and in a moment he stood to meet Ki, took the Winchester, and walked off into the dark. Jessie picked up her blanket and found a corner she liked.

"What are you thinking about?" she asked Ki. "Right now."

"Pancakes," he said at once. His mouth curved into a frown. "Hell, I don't even like pancakes."

"Yeah, well,"—Jessie turned her back to the fire—"it beats thinking about fish."

Ki moved off the ridge and down the slope, keeping in plain sight as he neared the camp so Hunter could see him clearly. The first touch of dawn turned the water slate-gray through the trees. Hunter had the horses saddled up and most of the gear loaded. He tightened a cinch and nodded.

"Any problems?"

"Nothing happened at all." They spoke in the quiet, easy tones of men in the morning.

"Easy watch. That's what we used to say in the army."

"Didn't know you were in."

"Longer than I wanted to be."

Jessie was still sleeping. "Where'd Natalia go?" Ki asked.

"Down there. To the water."

Ki nodded his thanks. He found her by the shore, looking out over the still darkened strait. Her long hair was loose and hung to her waist. She hugged her arms over her breasts as if she were cold.

"You all right?" He stopped behind her and held her. She laid her head against his shoulder.

"I had a bad dream," she told him. "I'm all right."

"I guess you're entitled to bad dreams."

She turned in his arms and faced him. "It was Maksutova. He was after me. He—Ki, you remember I told you once, the first day we met, that Maksutova wouldn't harm me. Remember? You looked at me real funny but didn't say anything."

"I thought it was a peculiar thing to say—considering."

Natalia lowered her eyes. "That's what scared me in the dream. You see he wouldn't hurt me. He thinks I belong to him."

"What?"

"I know it's crazy but it's true! I've always known it, the way he looks at me. He's never said a thing but I know it." Her eyes were haunted, full of old fears. "That's what the dream was about. Only it was more than just a dream. He let me go, Ki. I'm certain of that. Burke would kill him if he knew but I'm sure that it's true. He gave me a chance to get away. He murdered Nikolai and gave me a chance to run. He was telling me I was supposed to die, too, but he was letting me live so he could have me. He'll find me, Ki. In the dream that's how it happened!"

Ki held her close. "It's not going to happen, Natalia. I won't let it."

"I know you'll try," she said sadly, "I know you'll try, Ki."

"I'll do a hell of a lot more than try. Come on, let's get back." He started up the hill, holding her close into his shoulder and looking up at the campsite in the growing light. One of the horses snorted and stomped its foot and he heard Hunter speak to it softly. Then another sound reached him, the one that didn't belong; he stopped and stared up the hill as understanding reached him and told him what was wrong and how it would happen, that there was nothing he could do now to stop it.

The warning to Hunter and Jessie died on his lips as the shot cut harshly through the morning, ripping away the silence. The hill was suddenly alive with moving shadows, the sound of guns and shouting men. Ki thought he saw Hunter on his horse, the frightened animal pawing at the air. Then he was running for the water, tearing through the brush with Natalia in his arms.

Chapter 11

Ki raced swiftly along the shore, twisting and turning through the thick stand of trees. Natalia's eyes were wide with fear. He saw the scream beginning and roughly clamped his hand over her mouth. The shore was flat and rocky with no cover. Ki muttered a curse and kept going. He topped a small rise and plunged abruptly downhill, nearly falling and spilling the girl. A shower of loose gravel followed his path. The inlet below was choked with brush, a backwater cluttered with logs and tangled seaweed swept in from the straits. Gunfire echoed off the hill.

Ki ran through the brush and waded into the water. Natalia gasped at the sudden cold. He urged her to silence and pushed into deeper water. The stony bottom vanished almost at once. Natalia's face contorted in terror; he knew she was frightened of the water. He freed his hands from under her legs and she clasped her fingers frantically about his neck, digging her nails into his back. He made his way through the tangle, moving toward the neck of the inlet, keeping their heads low behind the shelter of the logs.

The gunfire stopped; no sound at all came from the campsite behind him. Suddenly, a man shouted to his right. Another answered and ran noisily through the trees. They'd turned their pursuit toward the water—in a moment they'd find the inlet and know where he and the girl had to be.

One of the saddled horses crashed through the trees along the shore, another fast on its heels. He risked a look and saw the first mount was his, the other Jessie's dark gelding. His heart sank at the sight. He told himself it meant nothing at all—Jessie would have taken the first horse at hand.

"Take it easy," he whispered to the girl. "Let your body relax in the water." Her chin was barely above the surface. Dark hair clung to her face and her enormous eyes darted wildly about.

"I'm freezing," she said. "God, Ki—!"

He rested a hand on her shoulder and peered cautiously around the edge of the log. They were a good twenty yards offshore, nearly in the center of the inlet. The morning sun was lost in a thick luminous haze over the mainland. He saw two gunmen appear, rifles held tightly in their hands. An Indian appeared an instant later, coming out of shadow and crouching low. Ki let out a breath. The Indian was one of the Hoonahs who'd sold them the horses. No big surprise. Still, Ki wondered how he'd found the camp so fast.

The Hoonah stopped and squatted on the ground, pointing at something he'd found. It was the place where Ki and Natalia had entered the water. The gunmen came suddenly alert. One levered a shell in his rifle. The Indian pointed out across the water. Ki didn't move a muscle. The Indian couldn't see him, but he would spot any motion at once.

The shots suddenly sounded in the distance—three shots from a rifle, evenly spaced and far away. The men on shore turned for an instant and Ki lowered himself quickly behind the log. He looked at Natalia and grinned. The girl didn't understand. What the hell was there to smile about? Ki's spirit soared. He was certain the shots were from Jessie. It was a signal. She was telling him she'd gotten away. It could be Burke's men, of course, letting the others know he'd found Jessie and Hunter. Ki knew better. It was Jessie, and she was free.

He waited, hoping the men would leave. Instead, they spread out along the shore, the Indian and one of the gunmen circling off to the right, the other running to the left. In a moment, the one on the left would spot them. When he did, he'd have a clear shot and wouldn't miss.

"Stay low," he whispered, "keep your nose above water. Don't get scared and raise your head." Natalia nodded and bit her lip.

There was nothing else to do. He couldn't afford to wait. Keeping as low as he could, he grasped the stubby branches under water and kicked his feet, pulling the log to him and backpedaling away from the jam. The men on shore spotted him at once. One shouted and fired at the log. Lead thunked into the water. The man found his target and his friend joined in. The bullets sounded like small hammers, pounding into the wood.

"Kick," Ki said tightly. "Use your legs and push!"

Natalia was frightened of the water, but the lead hitting inches above her head scared her more. She released Ki's neck and clung to the bottom of the log, grimly kicking at the water. Rifle fire from the shore quickened and Ki knew help had arrived. Burke's men loosed a steady volley at the log. Ki and Natalia were out of the inlet, a good ten yards offshore. Soon, Ki was sure, someone would think about running up on the ridge and taking a shot from there. Higher up, their heads would be visible behind the log.

"Keep going," he urged Natalia, "we're all right, we're okay." Natalia didn't believe him but she nodded and kept kicking.

A sound from the shore alerted him. Beneath the steady fire there was something else. He cocked his head and listened, told Natalia to hang on, and disappeared under the water. A good ten yards from the log he surfaced quickly, took a look inshore, and vanished before the men could bring their weapons around to catch him. It was just as he'd suspected from the noise. Two of the men had shed their clothes and jumped in the water. They were swimming as fast as they could after the log!

Ki surfaced next to Natalia and brushed water from his eyes. "Keep kicking," he told her. "I know you're tired but don't stop. Kick, then rest a few seconds, and start again."

Natalia blinked in alarm. "What are you going to do? You're not leaving me out here!"

"I'll be back. Just stay down."

"Ki, where are you going!"

Ki took a deep breath and disappeared. He skimmed along just below the surface until he spotted the first man up ahead, arms and legs churning the frothy water. He surfaced quickly and went deep, feeling the colder layer of water grip his body. His hand found the hilt of the *tanto* blade. He blew out air and let himself sink slowly in the water. Glancing up, he saw the man directly overhead. Kicking his arms and legs, he drove himself nearly to the surface, twisted on his back, and slashed out at the white belly. The water turned red. Ki made for deeper water, hearing the man screaming and thrashing behind him. Bullets made bright spears of light in the water. He surfaced next to Natalia; she turned on him and stared.

"My God, Ki, what's that? It's awful!"

Ki listened to the scream. "It's a damn fool with a bad idea," he told her. "Come on, we've got to get farther out." The man wouldn't die if they got to him quickly and stopped the bleeding. Ki hadn't tried to kill him—he wanted a lot of noise. He wasn't worried about the other man in the water, or anyone else jumping in.

At first they welcomed the sun, the heat that drew the chill out of their bodies. By late afternoon, the fierce ball of fire turned against them. Ki had long since stopped trying to guide the log in any direction. He had no strength for the task, and it was useless to fight the strong current. Chichagof Island was far to the west; for the moment, at least, they were heading away from Burke's men.

Ki was worried about Natalia. She was weakening fast; it was all she could do to hold on to the log. Thirst and exposure to the water and the searing rays of the sun were taking their toll. Dark clouds thickened in the west. Rain was already sweeping the coast. Distant thunder shook the sky and lightning brightened the flanks of the Chilkat peaks. If the rain came over the straits, the wind could churn the sea into a fury. And if the wind drove them away from the land...

"Ki—Ki, please!"

He opened his eyes quickly, startled to find he'd dozed. "Natalia, sorry—you all right?"

"Yes, Ki, I'm fine." A smile touched her weary features. "Look, Ki, over there. It's land!"

Ki shifted his grip on the log and squinted into the sun. A dark mass loomed directly ahead. It was a tree-covered island, more than likely a few miles across. Beyond, not far, was the mainland itself. He scanned the sky anxiously for the storm. The tail end was far off to the north. Ki kissed Natalia soundly, laughed, and pounded his fist against the log. "Come on, start kicking," he said, "I've had about all the boating I can take for one day."

Natalia shivered uncontrollably, huddled in her wet clothing, while Ki crouched down on his hands and knees in the small hollow. Again and again he struck the steel edge of a *shuriken* throwing star against stone. Sparks found his collection of dry grass. A sprig turned red, then blackened and died. Ki patiently tried again, blowing gently and cupping the grass in his palm.

A tiny flame appeared. Ki nursed it into life and added dry twigs one at a time. The fire snapped; a thin line of smoke rose to the branches overhead. In a moment, Ki had a respectable campfire going and a handy collection of wood.

"Oh, Lord, I never saw anything prettier in my life," Natalia sighed. She bent to the fire, stretching her hands inches from the flames.

Ki stripped the clammy shirt from his back and ran the loose arms under his belt. "Keep it alive," he told her. "I'll be back."

"Where are you going?"

"Shopping," Ki said wryly. "What's a picnic on an island without food?"

Natalia made a face. "Food would be fine. I'll settle for a gallon or two of water."

"I'll see what I can do."

He left her and walked uphill through the trees. The campsite was sheltered in a rocky draw near the center of the island. The trees would filter the smoke, and even after sundown the fire would be invisible to anyone who looked in that direction. Keeping to the cover of the forest, he circled the island from west to east.

The sun dropped below the high mountains and he knew the night would come upon them quickly. He kept going, cutting his circle short and moving back across the island toward the camp. Jessie hadn't been far from his thoughts all day. He told himself she was safe, that the evenly spaced shots had been hers.

The trees ended abruptly at an immense outcropping of stone, a sheer cliff that thrust like a wall out of the earth. He smelled them before he saw them. A grin creased his features. Birds—it was a rookery, a nesting place for seabirds. The evening meal would be eggs—all the eggs they could eat, mixed with the handful of wild onions he'd found on the edge of the woods.

When he saw her, a quick surge of excitement swept through his body; he drew in a breath and held it, savoring the secret pleasure of knowing she wasn't aware that he was there. He stood for a long moment, silent in the shadow of the trees. The fire was a warm glow in the hollow. She had stripped and spread her clothes on branches to dry.

Heat rose to Ki's face and he laughed at his fancy. He stepped into the clearing, making noise so she wouldn't be frightened. Natalia turned, saw him, and ran into his arms.

"I was worried. It got dark and you weren't here."

He held her bare shoulders and kissed her. "Most of the stores were closed. It took a little longer than I figured." He

93

opened the folds of his shirt and showed her the eggs and wild onions.

"You did it!" She squealed with delight. "You really did find food!"

"Come on," he told her, grasping her hand, "I've got a better surprise than that."

"Better? What could possibly be better?"

"You'll see." He led her past the clearing and into the trees. A few yards away, the forest was covered by glacier-worn boulders. Ki pulled Natalia to him and pointed. "That rain missed us this afternoon but it hit the island. There are a dozen or so little pools scattered about in the rocks. Take your pick."

"Oh, God, water. Real water!" Natalia's eyes went wide and she scampered tiptoe quickly over the rocks. She went to her knees and drank, cupping her hands and bringing the water to her mouth. The slim curve of her back arched in a bow. Ki studied her plush little bottom, the lean flanks of her thighs.

Natalia sprang to her feet. "Come on, I'm starved. I'm going to eat bird eggs till I pop!"

Chapter 12

Natalia found a thin flat stone, one surface curved like a bowl. She set the rock in the edge of the fire, propping it carefully with smaller stones. Ki stared hungrily at the flames, threatening to eat raw eggs if the makeshift stove didn't heat at once. Natalia told him to go right ahead. When the rock was finally ready, she broke the eggs in the hollow and scrambled them with a stick, tossing in the wild onions Ki had sliced up with his knife. They ate without speaking, scooping up the food with their hands, stopping only when the rock was scraped clean.

"I've eaten in a lot of fine places," Ki sighed. "This beats 'em all, hands down. Denver and San Francisco and New Orleans!"

"We finished everything off," Natalia said soberly. "You'll have to make another trip for breakfast." She stared into the fire a long time. "What are we going to do, Ki? We can't stay here, I know that."

"We couldn't, even if we wanted to," he told her. "The

rocks will soak up most of that water by morning; the sun will take care of the rest. We'll have a morning drink and that's all. We'll have to do something after that."

"What?" She stared at him a moment, alarm spreading over her features. "Oh, no, not that log. Ki, I don't think I can do it!"

"Maybe we can lash three or four logs together. It'd be a little better than one."

"Lash them together with what?"

"I don't know. Vines or something. We'll figure it out in the morning." He stood and ran his hands over the trousers and shirt he'd braced next to the fire. Both were still wet. Natalia's shirt was dry; he held it to the fire, draped it over her shoulders.

"Mmm, that feels wonderful." Natalia closed her eyes and sighed. Ki sat down and put his arm around her shoulder. She touched his bare thigh and ran a finger to his knee.

She twisted in his arms, letting the shirt slide off her shoulders, lifted her face, and kissed the hollow of his neck. "If you believe this, then I do, too."

He touched her chin and turned her mouth up to his. Her glacier-blue eyes blurred with tears. He kissed her eyes gently, tasting salt and feeling the brush of her lashes against his lips. She made a little sound in her throat and squirmed her body comfortably against him. He looked past her shoulder to the fire and followed the sleek curve of her back. Flame turned her skin to copper. Her hair was a dark veil against her flesh. The narrow circle of her waist flared to a firmly rounded bottom. She had draped one leg across his thigh and he could feel the hard little mound against his skin. Her hands snaked under his arms and grasped his back, pushing him gently to the ground. She brought her hands to his cheeks and gave him a long, lazy smile. The hot points of her breasts smouldered against his chest. Ki slid his hands along her back and clutched the twin mounds of her hips. Natalia began to move in a slow, easy rhythm along his thigh. An intense little frown creased her brow; tendons went taut in her throat. The downy nest between her legs was like a furnace. Her mouth fell open in a silent cry of delight; her lithe young body began to shudder as she ground herself wantonly against him.

Natalia's eyes went wide but Ki knew she couldn't see him. His hands kneaded the lovely swell of her bottom, drawing her to him again and again. Suddenly, Natalia gave a harsh, strangled cry of joy. Her hot little mound spasmed against him and she stiffened in his arms. Ki dug his hands savagely into her hips as the fiery waves of release wracked her body.

"Oh, God!" Natalia gasped and fell limply into his arms. "I never did anything like that in my life. I never even thought about pleasuring myself on a man."

Ki kissed her gently, tasting the fine pearls of moisture on her brow. "And how did you like this pleasure?"

"I like it. I like it very much."

Without warning, he grasped her shoulders and twisted her off of his chest onto her back. She squealed in protest as he grabbed her wrists and pinned her solidly to the earth. Natalia's slender form thrashed beneath him. Ki savored the heat of her flesh, the sharp, animal scent of her body. He saw her again in his mind, as he had seen her from the shadow of the trees. The memory stiffened him even more.

"My hands," she whispered, "let go of my hands. Please!"

Ki released her at once. She let her hands slide up her sides to cup her breasts. The tips of her fingers caressed her nipples. She tossed back her head and groaned with delight, lips stretched tight against her teeth. Her fingers kneaded the firm mounds of flesh, drawing the hard nipples into sharp points of scarlet.

She squeezed her breasts in her palms, offering them to his mouth. Ki stroked the silken tips, flipping the coral buds with his tongue. He sucked the spicy nipples again and again, marveling at the way her ripe young breasts were both delightfully firm and satiny soft. Natalia groaned and threw her head from side to side. Dark hair whipped against Ki's face. Now his slightest touch brought a cry from the girl's lips. Her breath came in rapid little bursts and Ki knew she trembled on the sweet edge of release. He drew her breasts firmly into his mouth, letting the nipples pass gently between his teeth. Natalia shrieked and raked her nails across his back. Her body arched in a bow as the orgasm shook her.

Natalia closed her eyes and gave a grateful sigh of pleasure.

"Don't go to sleep yet," Ki said. "We're not finished, girl."

"Huh? What do you mean?" Natalia stared in alarm.

Ki let his lips trail down the length of her body to her treasure. He kneeled between her legs and kissed one thigh and then the other.

"Oh my—God!" Natalia's slim form went rigid.

Ki let his eyes feast on the long stretch of her legs, the delicate swell of her belly rising to the curve of her ribs. He spread her thighs gently with his hands, baring the soft and downy nest. He parted the feathery curls and let his fingers briefly rest. Ki taunted the silken flesh, circled the moist crown of her delight, brushed it lightly but never near enough. Natalia cried out with joy. Ki withdrew his touch and kissed her sleek petals with the tip of his tongue. Natalia gasped and sucked in a breath. Her bottom jerked off the ground and trembled against him. Ki caressed the lovely hollow, teasing the tender flesh with his mouth. Silken down tickled his cheeks. He kissed her honeyed self, barely touching her at all. Natalia groaned with lazy pleasure. Suddenly, without warning, he thrust his tongue deeply.

Natalia clawed the earth with her fingers. Tendons corded in her thighs and her pelvis jerked in rapid little spasms. Ki thrust deeper and deeper, searching the satin smoothness of her. The musky scent of her flesh heightened his arousal; his loins cried out for release. He could feel the long columns of her legs against his cheeks. He stroked her again and again, moving closer to the crown of her pleasure. He felt her orgasm mounting, trembling through her veins.

Natalia gave a ragged cry of delight. Her body jerked uncontrollably, then fell back limply to the ground. Ki drew her into his arms. She stared at him in wonder, drawing air deeply into her lungs. A vein pulsed rapidly in her throat.

"I never felt anything like that before," she told him.

"You know how to give that pleasure," Ki said. "I ought to know."

"Yes, but that is different," she exclaimed. "I didn't know completely what a man could do to a woman. My God—what a pleasure!"

She left his arms and sprang to her feet, scampering lightly to the fire. Flame danced on the smooth length of her thighs, the slender columns of her wickedly lovely legs. Her flesh still glistened from their love. She bent to warm her hands, offering him a view of her firm and lovely bottom.

"Natalia," he said evenly, "will you come back here, please?"

He came to his feet and reached her in a single motion, grasped her waist, and swept her off her feet. She shrieked with delight and flailed her legs in the air. Ki laid her firmly on her belly and lifted her bottom off the ground. Natalia convulsed in laughter. Ki kneeled between her legs until his thighs touched the plush swell of her hips. Natalia gasped and dug her knees into the earth. Holding her waist firmly between his hands, he thrust his member deeply inside her.

Natalia cried out and threw back her head. He drew her roughly to him with his hands, thrust her away, then jerked her back once more. His loins slammed hard against her bottom, forcing bursts of air from her lungs. He drove himself inside her again and again, pounding her relentlessly, feeling his member swell with every thrust. His body filled with her warmth, bringing him ever closer to the storm that would carry him away. Natalia's body shuddered. He could feel her orgasm mounting, the silken walls throbbing about his shaft.

"Now, Ki," she begged. "Oh yes, *now!*"

Ki gave a strangled cry and filled her like a flood. Natalia thrashed under his grip. Ki exploded again and again, one spasm of pleasure coming swiftly on the heels of another. Natalia groaned and went limp, sagging under his hands. Ki lowered her gently to the ground. She twisted on her back and raised her arms to welcome him. Ki covered her face and breasts with kisses. Her flesh was slick with moisture, dotted with a million tiny pearls. Her enormous blue eyes closed to slits. She gave him a lazy grin and made a sound deep in her throat.

"Lady," Ki said evenly, "there is nothing about loving you don't know."

Natalia's eyes sparkled with pleasure. "All I know is that I have been loved extremely well. Do you suppose there are still more things that I can learn? Am I good enough to merit another lesson?"

Ki moaned and threw an arm across his eyes. "Sometime, perhaps. Not now."

Natalia laughed and thrust her hand between his legs. Ki lifted her thigh and slapped her bottom soundly. He came to his feet and held out his hand. She grasped his wrist and joined him, following him back through the trees. The water standing in the hollows of the rocks was cool and sweet. They cupped their hands and drank, leaving enough for the morning. Ki gathered more wood and carried it back to camp. While he built up the fire for the night, Natalia shook the dried leaves and twigs from their clothes.

Ki woke several times and looked up at the trees and the dark sky beyond. The night was full of sounds, but none that didn't belong. There were insects and birds, the steady sigh of wind in the high branches. Once, he heard something off in the brush, rose quickly, and walked into the darkness to stand silently under a tree. In a moment he saw some small animal nosing through the carpet of leaves.

He walked back to camp and stirred the fire, then eased back down beside Natalia. She moaned in her sleep, made a face, and draped her leg across his thigh. Ki grinned.

He woke at the unfamiliar sound, jumped up quickly, and reached for the *tanto* blade. The first touch of dawn bled through the trees. Two Indians stood just inside the clearing, past the fire. The first looked at him with no expression at all. The other aimed his tautly strung bow, its arrow pointed directly at Ki's head.

Chapter 13

Ki didn't move a muscle.

"Natalia," he said evenly, "wake up and be very still. Don't scream or anything—just lie there. All right?" He spoke to the girl but his eyes didn't waver from the Indians. They met his gaze with dark, unsmiling faces.

"What is it, Ki?" Natalia groaned, "I'm not even—oh, Lord!"

"Easy," Ki said sharply, "don't show them you're afraid."

"How am I—how am I going to do that?"

"Just do it."

Natalia forced herself to look at the Indians. "Hello," she said feebly. "Good morning."

The Indian without a weapon muttered to his friend. The man relaxed his pull on the bow but kept his arrow at the ready. His companion uttered a harsh command and raised his fist. The gesture was clear enough.

"He wants us to get up," said Ki. "Do it real slow."

Ki and Natalia came to their feet. The Indians backed off

a step. The bowman raised his weapon again and aimed it at Ki's chest. The other man walked cautiously around behind Ki. He removed the *tanto* blade from Ki's belt, then found the *shuriken* throwing stars in the pocket of his jacket. He frowned curiously at the circles of steel, gingerly touched the razored points, and showed the objects to his friend. The man with the bow looked suspiciously at Ki. The first man pointed toward the shore and gestured with his head.

"He wants us to go with him," said Ki.

"Thank you," Natalia said dryly. "I'm glad you're so good with languages."

"You're the Alaskan," Ki reminded her, "you talk to him."

Natalia didn't answer. They walked ahead of the Indians through the trees. Seagulls squawked along the rocky beach, fighting over a salmon that had washed up on the shore. Ki glanced up and saw a bald eagle soaring high in the gray morning sky. He guessed its wingspan was a good seven feet. The Indians looked like the ones he'd seen in Sitka. They were much more confident and self-assured than the people of the Hoonah village on Chichagof Island. Instead of trade clothes, they wore their own dress—loose trousers and goat's-wool jackets in yellow and black geometric patterns.

The cedar canoe was pulled ashore along the beach. The taller, unarmed Indian stopped and pointed.

"Baidarka," he said shortly, *"baidarka!"*

Natalia drew in a breath. "Ki, that's not Tlingit; it's Russian! It's our word for kayak. That's not exactly a kayak but that's what he means."

"Come on," Ki said grimly, "let's get in the boat."

The village lay in a sheltered cove on the mainland. The awesome Chilkat Range loomed in the west, trailing off north as far as the eye could see. A cluster of women and children met the boat and followed Ki and Natalia from the shore, chattering and pointing at the pair.

The Tlingits led them from the beach to a cluster of large, gable-roofed dwellings set in a grove of Sitka spruce.

The Indians signaled Ki and Natalia to halt before the largest house in the village. A tall totem stood before the door. Eyes and grinning mouths full of teeth stared at Ki from the elaborately carved pole. At the top was the figure of a raven in flight.

The taller of the two Tlingits disappeared inside the house. The bowman kept a watchful eye on Ki and Natalia. In a moment, there were forty or fifty Indians in a circle around the pair.

"They don't look happy," said Ki. "If you know anything about these people, now's the time to tell me."

"I know a lot about them," Natalia said darkly, "but nothing that's going to be much help. They hate the white man, especially Russians, because we were here first. They have good reason, of course. You notice the difference between these people and the Hoonahs?"

"Yes, I noticed."

"They're farther from Sitka. They trade with the whites sometimes but they're not afraid of them. Not much, anyway."

Ki glanced at the scowling faces. "You didn't have to tell me that."

Natalia started to speak. The Indian who'd brought them to the village came out of the house. He stood aside respectfully and lowered his head. Another man came out of the dark interior. He was taller than the other Tlingits and had to stoop to get through the door. He was a broad, heavily muscled man approximately in his early sixties. He wore an elaborate headdress that looked like a raven, and an apronlike robe with painted figures on the front and tassles on the shoulders. He let his eyes rest on Natalia a long moment, then turned to face Ki. Finally, he gestured to someone in the crowd. A gaunt, sad-eyed young man came forward, listened, nodded, and walked up to Ki.

"My name is Samuel," he said in perfect English. "That is not my real name, but it is what you may call me. They will not let me have my real name back. He is Chief Yaska. He wants to know what you were doing sleeping on his island. No one is supposed to go there." His eyes darted furtively to his right. "Now, this is from me, not him. You are in a great deal

103

of trouble. He doesn't like anyone white. It is clear that you are not completely white, but that won't help you here. I hope you have some good reason for being where you were. Whatever it is, I doubt if it's good enough."

Ki let out a breath. "My name is Ki, and this is Natalia. Please tell the chief we had no idea the island was his. We did not go there on purpose. We were fleeing from some men on Chichagof Island and floated there on a log."

Samuel looked distressed. "You are criminals? Is that why you were running away?"

"No, the men who are after us are the criminals, not us. They murdered this woman's uncle in Sitka. They want to kill her, too."

"Why?"

"Because she was very brave and fought them," Ki lied solemnly. "The man who killed her uncle is shamed by her courage. This is why he wants her dead."

"This is all true?" Samuel looked narrowly at Ki. "It sounds like a story from a white man's book."

"Yes, it is all true," Ki assured him.

Samuel turned to the chief. He spoke for a long time in the short, clipped syllables of the Tlingit tongue. The crowd murmured and nodded. Chief Yaska silenced them with a look. His mouth curled in distaste and he barked out a reply to Samuel. Samuel faced Ki again and glanced at Natalia.

"I was afraid of this," he said tightly. "Chief Yaska says he admires your courage. A daughter of his would have done the same thing. Nevertheless, you had no business on his island."

"We didn't go to his island on purpose," Natalia protested. "Ki told you that!"

Samuel shrugged. "Chief Yaska doesn't care how you got there. He says whites think they can go anywhere they wish. They can, of course, but Chief Yaska doesn't like to believe this. I told him that you were in trouble."

"Now what?" Ki asked. "What's he going to do?"

Samuel wet his lips and stared at the sky. "I don't know. He will talk to the *icht* first."

"The what? Who's that?"

"A witch, a sorceress. Her name is Ka-shu-da-klock."

"Oh, Lord," Natalia moaned, "I've heard of her, Ki. She's crazy. She's got hair six feet long and she's ugly as sin. Even the Tlingits in Sitka are afraid of her."

Ki muttered under his breath. "And what's this witch likely to say? Or maybe I don't want to know."

Samuel nodded. "Ka-shu-da-klock doesn't like whites, either."

Chief Yaska shouted angrily at Samuel. The young Tlingit turned quickly, listened, and spoke to Ki. "The round things that are sharp, with blades like a saw. He wants to know what they are for."

"The *shuriken*. Tell him they are weapons."

Samuel passed Ki's words along. Chief Yaska's face clouded. He loosed an angry string of venom in Ki's direction. The crowd responded at once, yelling and shaking their fists.

"Now what did I do?" Ki said darkly.

Samuel looked frightened. "He says you are a liar. He knows the little circles are not weapons. He says you wish to make a fool of him in front of his people."

Ki's eyes darted past Samuel as several of the Tlingits moved toward him from the crowd. He shifted his feet on the earth. Natalia shouted a warning. Ki turned and caught a man with a painted wooden club coming at him; he kicked out savagely and buried his foot in the man's gut. Another Indian took him from behind, wrapped his arms around Ki's legs, and spilled him to the ground. Ki rolled and kicked free, slashed the man hard across his face with the edge of his palm, and came to his feet. A big warrior charged him from the left, arms spread wide like a bear. Ki let him come. The Tlingit swung wildly with his fists. Ki ducked under the blow, stiffened his fingers, and thrust his hand at the man's throat like a knife. The man went limp and sagged to the earth.

Ki turned, sensing another Indian before he saw him. The warrior hefted a long harpoon in his hand, brought his arm forward in a blur, and tossed the weapon at Ki with all his strength. There was no time to think—Ki's body reacted on its own. His knees and waist bent to the left while his right arm darted in that direction. The harpoon flashed by inches from his chest. Ki caught the shaft in his fist, letting the momentum of the weapon turn him around. He shifted his grip as he moved and hurled the harpoon at Yaska's feet. Yaska's mouth dropped open. He stared at the weapon still quivering between his legs.

A warrior broke the sudden silence, shouting a war cry and waving his weapon over his head. Yaska raised his hand. The warrior stopped.

"Tell him I am not a liar," Ki said flatly. "Tell him it is he who insults my honor." Samuel was struck dumb. *"Tell him!"* Ki said hoarsely.

Samuel swallowed and repeated Ki's words. Yaska looked at Ki. His dark eyes smoldered with anger. Ki stalked boldly up to the chief, stopped, and held his palm out flat. Yaska's gaze never wavered. He dropped the two *shuriken* in Ki's hand. Ki stepped back and looked to his left. A clay pot hung from the eaves of a house across the clearing. Ki dropped in a crouch; his hand moved too fast to follow. The first throwing star clipped the woven cord that held the pot. The second shattered the vessel before it hit the ground.

A low moan rose from the crowd. Ki walked calmly to the house, dug the steel weapons from the wood, and dropped them in the pocket of his jacket.

Chief Yaska spoke again. He didn't look at Ki. Samuel nodded. Sweat peppered his brow and his face was drained of color. "Chief Yaska says you are his guests," he told Ki. "You will stay in the dwelling of his third son. Food and drink will be brought to you. You will not come out of the house unless you are told."

"And then what?"

Samuel blinked in dismay. "Will you please not ask more questions? He is very angry at me, and I have nothing at all to do with this!"

Ki paced back and forth in the large, high-roofed dwelling. The house was clean, but the odor of fish was overwhelming. Hundreds of dried salmon hung from the rafters, just above the height of a normal Tlingit. Ki had to duck as he walked.

"I'm not sure I did the right thing," Ki said soberly.

"What are you talking about?"

"Throwing that harpoon at the chief. I was trying to get his respect. I couldn't think of anything else."

"Well, it worked, didn't it? Besides, he was very impressed with those—whatever they are."

"*Shuriken*. He was impressed, but he was also madder than hell."

"Ki, don't worry about it now. You're right. There was nothing else you could have done. They were about that close to killing us on the spot."

Ki started to answer. He turned as one edge of the blanket slipped off its pegs and Samuel ducked inside.

"What are they doing," Ki asked anxiously. "How does it look, Samuel?"

"I don't know," Samuel said evenly. "Yaska doesn't like you. You can't tell what he's going to do."

"Maybe I could give him a gift of some kind."

"A gift of what? Anything you have, Yaska can take if he wants."

"Samuel!" Natalia sprang eagerly to her feet. "Samuel, I just thought of something. Have you ever heard of a man named Hiram Platte? He was a friend of the Tlingits, a man who—"

"Yes, of course." Samuel looked surprised. "I know of Mr. Platte. I have even seen him. I was a Presbyterian once. This is how I learned to speak English. I went to the mission school in Wrangell. What of Mr. Platte?"

Ki could see where Natalia was headed. "Mr. Platte is dead, Samuel. He was murdered by the same men who are after us. That's what we were doing on Chief Yaska's island."

"Samuel," Ki asked, "is Yaska talking to that witch? Is she here in your village now?"

"Ka-shu-da-klock is here." Samuel looked at the floor. "She has told Yaska that you are possessed by evil spirits. She says you should be killed."

"Oh, Lord!" Natalia dug her fingers in Ki's arm.

"That doesn't mean Yaska will do it," Samuel told her. "He

listens to Ka-shu-da-klock with respect. But in the end he will do what he wants."

"And what do you think that'll be?" Ki asked.

"Who can say? As I have told you, it is hard to say what a chief will do." Samuel turned as voices approached the door. A warrior jerked the blanket aside and spoke rapidly to Samuel. Samuel turned to face Ki and Natalia. "Yaska has decided. He will not kill you. You will be released."

"Oh, that's wonderful!" Natalia breathed a long sigh of relief.

"Wait, please." Samuel looked at the rafters. "You will be taken to the top of the mountains. Your clothes and weapons will be taken from you. You will have no food—"

"What?" Ki went rigid. He stared past Samuel at the cold, forbidding peaks of the Chilkat Range. "Damn it, that's not setting us free and he knows it," Ki raged. "We'll die up there!"

Samuel's broad features betrayed no expression at all. "I did not say you wouldn't die, Ki. I said Yaska would not kill you. I am to tell you that he greatly admires your courage and your fighting skills. I am to say that it would shame him if you died at the hands of his people. I am to tell you that it gives him great joy to set you free."

Chapter 14

The Tlingits marched them along the beach for a half hour, then turned abruptly north through a thick stand of spruce. At the top of a high rise Ki could look back and see the shore below, the island where they'd slept, and the dark blur of Chichagof Island. The whole village had turned out for the occasion. Chief Yaska led the way in his ceremonial robes. Behind him, surrounding Ki and Natalia, were warriors bristling with weapons. The women and children brought up the rear. Everyone was laughing. The women carried plenty of food and drink.

Three miles past the village, Ki got his first look at Ka-shu-da-klock. She leaped out of the bushes, screamed, shook her stick, and disappeared. Natalia gripped Ki's arm. The Tlingits groaned and hid their faces. Ki decided the old woman was as ugly as Natalia had described. Her face was hideously scarred and smeared with dabs of green and yellow paint. Filthy robes were tangled in the mat of long black hair that trailed behind her.

A few minutes later, the witch appeared again. She shouted and stomped, then vanished into the trees. Five minutes later she was back—and five minutes after that. Each time she made an appearance, the Indians rolled their eyes in awe, as if they'd never seen her before.

Natalia said, "I'd like someone to explain just how we are going to survive up there in the snow. With no clothes and no food."

"We're not," Ki said flatly. "We're going to get out of here, Natalia, before we get close to that mountain."

"Good. How do we plan to do that?"

"I don't know. Just be ready."

"I'm ready right now."

"We'll have to try it before we get out of the forest," Ki said thoughtfully. "We'd never lose them in the open. Yaska won't take the women and children up past the tree line. When we get to open ground, he'll take us up to the snow with a few warriors. That's when he'll stop pretending to set us free." He glanced meaningfully at the girl. "Natalia, I don't believe for a minute he's going to just leave us up there. He'll have to make sure. He'll tie us up before he leaves us in the cold— probably as soon as we get out of sight from the others. We'll have to make a break before that."

Natalia bit her lip. "Ki . . . what if he decides to–to do away with us before he leaves us on the mountain? He could, you know."

"Of course, he could. We're not going to wait and find out, are we?"

Late in the afternoon, the path grew steeper through the wooded hills. The icy peaks of the Chilkats blotted out the sky to the east. They were close—much closer than Ki liked. Soon, the women and children would make camp and wait for the men to go up to the mountains.

Ki knew he could make it. He could kill or disable enough of the Tlingits and be gone before they could stop him. He had known it from the start, from the moment Samuel told them Yaska was taking them to the mountains. He could get away from the Tlingits, take Natalia with him to the safety of the woods. Ten minutes later they'd have her. He'd have to run at her pace and that wasn't good enough. The Indians would get them both. He couldn't take Natalia and run, and he wouldn't leave without her. He knew what he had to do. There was nothing else left and that was that.

Yaska brought his party to a halt at the top of a high ridge overlooking the inland sea. A valley and another stretch of forest lay ahead. Beyond was the first granite spur of the mountains.

It has to be now. He won't take the women and children any farther than the valley.

"Natalia, stay close to me," Ki said. "I want you about six inches away, all right?"

Natalia read the tension in his voice. "Ki, what is it—what's wrong?"

"Nothing's wrong. Just do it." She started to protest but Ki was already striding up the path toward Yaska. A big Tlingit warrior stepped in his way.

"Samuel," Ki called out, "tell Chief Yaska I must speak to him at once."

Samuel turned. He was standing a few feet from the old man. He looked curiously at Ki and turned to Yaska. A moment later, Yaska frowned and shook his head.

"Chief Yaska says there is nothing he wishes to hear you say."

"Tell him the woman and I want to show our respect. Tell him that I am a Presbyterian, and that I wish to renounce my faith before we go up the mountain. He has shown me that his gods and the magic of Ka-shu-da-klock are far greater than anything the white preachers offer. Tell him I wish to say these things and bow before him in front of his people."

Samuel's eyes widened in surprise. "This is so? You truly wish to do such a thing?"

"I do, Samuel. Tell him now. Tell him exactly as I said it."

"Ki, what are you doing?" Natalia spoke without moving her lips.

111

Ki ignored her. Samuel turned to Yaska again. Ki held his breath. He could almost see the wheels turning in the chief's head. The somber lines of his face suddenly eased into a satisfied grin. He liked the idea of getting back at the white man in front of his people. He liked the idea a lot. He spoke in rapid syllables to Samuel.

"Chief Yaska says you may approach him," Samuel told Ki. "He says he will allow you to renounce your faith, if you will accept his in turn."

"Tell him that's fine with me," said Ki.

Samuel spoke to Yaska and Yaska shouted a command to his warriors. The Tlingits stepped aside to let Ki and Natalia through. Yaska raised his hands over his head and spoke for a long time to his people. His voice thundered through the hills. Ki needed no translation. The Tlingits cheered and Yaska beamed. Ki saw Ka-shu-da-klock edging up to the chief, glaring suspiciously at Ki and trying to get Yaska's attention. Yaska pushed her away.

Ki approached the chief. Yaska gave Ki a scornful grin. "Bow to him," Ki told Natalia under his breath. "Bow to him and stay close to me."

"I'm scared, Ki. Whatever this is, I don't like it."

"Shut up," Ki said calmly. "Just do it."

Ki stopped before Yaska, staying a respectful three feet away. Yaska raised his chin proudly and crossed his arms across his chest. Ki bowed, bending from the waist. As he straightened, he thrust his left foot forward and slammed it to the ground, swept his right arm up in a blur, and circled the chief's neck, jerking Yaska against his chest. Yaska cried out as Ki snaked his own *tanto* blade from the chief's belt and pressed the edge against the Indian's throat. The Tlingit warriors started for Ki, then froze.

"If anyone tries to come up behind, you sing out," Ki told Natalia.

"Oh, my God," Natalia moaned.

"Tell them if they move their chief is dead," Ki called out to Samuel. "We're leaving and he's going with us. If they follow, I'll cut off his head."

112

Samuel stared. His whole body shook with fear.

"*Tell* them," Ki blurted, "and you'd damn well better make them believe it, Samuel!"

The young Tlingit turned and spoke. The warriors growled and shook their weapons. Ki loosened his choke hold on the chief, bent his arm to the center of his back, and walked him awkwardly down the path back to the trees. A warrior took a step toward Ki and Ki thrust his knife hard against Yaska's throat. Yaska yelled and the Tlingit backed off.

"You could have told me what you were going to do," Natalia said darkly. "I thought I was going to pass out."

"That's why I didn't tell you. Just keep your eyes open. I want to know what those Indians are doing." Ki guided Yaska down the path the way they'd come. Yaska's eyes blazed; he spat a string of Tlingit words in Ki's direction, and Ki had a good idea what they meant. He found a short knife in the chief's clothing and passed it to Natalia. His two *shuriken* were there as well and he dropped them in the pocket of his jacket. On the hill above, the witch Ka-shu-da-klock leaped out of the brush and made herself visible again. She screamed at the warriors and shook her stick at Ki. It was clear enough she was urging them to fight—chief or no chief.

"They're following," said Natalia. "They're keeping their distance but they are not stopping, Ki."

"They might," Ki said tightly, "if that crazy old lady would leave them alone. I should've figured she'd be a—"

The harsh crack of a rifle chopped off his words. Ki stopped and stared down the hill as another shot followed the first. He saw them, then, racing wildly up the path—three, then four of the Tlingits Yaska had left behind in the village. One suddenly screamed and threw up his arms as a bullet caught him in the back.

"*Ki!*" Natalia pointed shakily down the hill. Ki saw it—a cutter riding at anchor off the shore. It was two, maybe three miles back. A terrified Indian ran past him; he didn't look back or wonder what was happening to his chief. The Indians behind Ki shook their weapons and yelled, then turned as one and fled in the other direction. Ki released Yaska and pushed him roughly away.

"Go on, get out of here!" he said. Yaska glared, glanced down the hill, and turned and ran.

Natalia stood frozen, her face twisted in fear. Ki grabbed her arm and jerked her roughly off the path to the cover of the trees. Lifting her up in his arms, he scrambled down the steep, brush-covered slope to the thicket below. The forest was dark, the tall trunks set closely together. The ground was covered with ferns and choking vines. Ki stopped and set Natalia on her feet.

"Run," he told her calmly, "keep a good easy pace. Don't wear yourself out."

"All right . . . I'm all right . . ."

"I know you are," he said. "Let's go. Keep running."

Natalia started off through the woods and Ki followed. More shots came from the pathway above. Maybe Burke's men hadn't seen them; if they chased the Tlingits long enough, he and Natalia would have a chance. If they didn't . . . He had seen the look in her eyes, followed her glance down the hill, and spotted the men working their way up the rise. It was too far away to be sure but he knew it couldn't be anyone else. Natalia knew it, too. The man leading the others up from the ship was Maksutova or his twin.

Marcus Hunter lay silently on the edge of the high ridge. The thick stand of yellow cedar masked the rim of the granite wall; the gnarled roots of the trees twisted precariously into space. The roots and low branches sheltered Hunter from the eyes of the men below. He turned for an instant as Jessie bellied up beside him, then took up his vigil again.

"What are they doing?" she said softly. "Anything different?"

"Having breakfast," Hunter growled, "can't you smell it? Coffee, bacon—"

"That's enough," said Jessie. She moved up closer, using her elbows to pull her along. She could look right down into the camp some fifty feet below. There was no wind and the

114

smoke from the fire rose straight up in a line. Jessie could have leaned out and touched it. Four men squatted around the fire. The horses were off to the left. There were nine men in camp, and that meant five were off somewhere else. Jessie looked at Hunter and Hunter guessed her thoughts.

"I've got no idea what's so interesting over there," he whispered. "There's a narrow inlet to the right—that tree's in your way but I can see it from here. They've been wandering down there and back in twos and threes since just after sunup."

Jessie shrugged. Raising slightly, she could see a strip of gray on the horizon. Hunter had told her it was the mainland, but Jessie thought it could just as easily have been a bank of low clouds. Whatever it was, it seemed impossibly far away. A near endless stretch of water lay between the tip of Chichagof Island and the land to the north. Twenty miles or a thousand— it didn't make a hell of a lot of difference. There was no way to get off the island.

It had happened too fast, only seconds between the beginning and the end. She had heard the shots and come quickly out of sleep, turned to see Hunter pull himself up in the saddle and shout out her name. The frightened animal pawed air and struck its hooves against stone. Hunter thrust out his arm and Jessie took it, pulling herself quickly up behind him. The other horses were gone. A bullet hummed close to her head. Hunter dug his heels in hard and they were out from under the cliff and into the open. *Ki, Ki—damn it all, where are you!*

If Hunter had run before them and played the fox, Burke's men would have had them. They were ready, waiting for that. Hunter let them chase him along the flats near the shore. Jessie jerked the Winchester from the saddle and fired off three shots for Ki. Hunter hit a slab of hard granite to cover his tracks, then forced the horse up the slope into the dense forests and treacherous glacial rifts. Instead of running he went wide and came up behind his pursuers. They had split their forces, leaving half the men behind. Jessie could hear them firing off to her right and guessed they were after Ki.

A half hour out, Hunter knew they'd gotten a break. Whoever

115

had tracked them to the camp and surprised them wasn't on their trail anymore. The cutback trick wouldn't have fooled a man who really knew his business.

By late afternoon, the rest of Burke's men caught up with their companions. Hunter spotted the tracker. It was a Hoonah, one of the men who'd sold them the horses. It was too late then for the Indian to do his job. Jessie and Hunter were behind and above their pursuers, following them to the north. When the men made camp that night, Jessie and Hunter slept right above them.

"You know how that son of a bitch did it?" Hunter said shortly. He clenched his fists and glared down at the camp, the morning sun turning his face to copper. "Damn that little bastard!"

"What are you talking about?" asked Jessie.

"That tracker—the Hoonah. I've been wondering how he did it. It's as simple as it can be. He trailed us from the minute we left his village. Saw us bed down and ran back to sell what he knew to Burke's men. The Hoonahs knew we were on the run; it wasn't hard to figure."

Jessie scarcely heard him. She stared past the branches and saw the white sails and the dark smoke of the sleek cutter rounding the point, heading for the inlet to her left. An enormous figure stood in the bow, clinging to the rigging and gazing toward the shore. Something cold touched the back of Jessie's neck. The man couldn't see her, couldn't possibly know she was there. Yet, she felt as if he were staring up at the ridge, looking directly into her eyes.

Chapter 15

"Mark—look there!" Jessie's fingers tightened on Hunter's arm. "I've never seen him before, but that's got to be Maksutova!"

"It's him all right." Hunter muttered. Cold anger edged his words. "You can't miss the bastard."

"Then he wasn't with the men who hit our camp."

"I didn't much figure he was. If Maksutova had been there, we'd likely be skinned and hung out to dry by now." Hunter frowned in thought. "Burke must have had him holding the fort in Sitka while he took off for Yakutat Bay. You can bet that galled Maksutova. He's up here now, Jessie, because they told him you got off of Baranof Island." Hunter laughed in his throat. "Wait till he finds out his boys messed up twice. I'm glad it's not me that has to tell him."

The ship dropped anchor in the narrow bay. It was a trim, two-masted cutter; a tall stack belched a pall of black smoke. Jessie and Hunter watched as three men from the camp walked down to meet the ship. It was clear they were in no big hurry.

Two of the men hung back and let the other do the talking. Maksutova listened a long moment. Then, without warning, his big hands shot up from his sides and he gripped the man by the throat, lifting his body off the ground. Jessie sucked in a breath. Even from a distance, she could hear the giant's bellow of rage. His victim clawed the air and kicked out helplessly with his legs. Maksutova held the man straight out in his strong hands. The man's limbs jerked feebly, then his body went limp. Maksutova let him fall. He was clearly dead, but the giant wasn't finished. He walked around the body and kicked it savagely with his boots again and again. Blood began to soak the man's clothing.

"My—*God!*" Jessie felt bile rise to her throat. She tried to look away but the horror held her eyes. Finally, Maksutova stooped and grabbed one of the man's legs and dragged the ruined figure to the nearest tree. Lifting the man by his shoulders, he jammed the head in the crook of a branch and let the body hang free. Jessie was certain there wasn't a bone unbroken in the man's body. She looked at Hunter and saw his eyes were dark with rage; his jaw was clenched tight and a vein throbbed in his throat.

Below, the camp suddenly came to life. Maksutova stalked along the shore bawling instructions. A gunman got in his way and the giant cuffed him aside, sent him sprawling. The man came to his feet, shook his head, and stumbled away.

"He's got 'em stirred up good," Hunter said softly. He offered Jessie a grim smile. "Looks like our easy living is done. They're going to be all over the place now."

"You think we'd be better off somewhere else? Makes sense to me to stay right where we are."

"You're right. We don't leave here unless we have to. It's the last place they'll—" Hunter stopped and nodded past the camp. "Hey, Maksutova's leaving again. Now what's he up to?"

Jessie watched as Maksutova climbed into the small dory and let the crewmen row him back to the cutter. Moments later, the engines throbbed into life and the ship weighed anchor. Once more, smoke billowed from the tall stack and the cutter leaned to port and made way. White sails were unfurled and the vessel moved rapidly into the strait.

"He's going east," Jessie said under her breath. "Toward the mainland and those mountains. Why would he do that, Mark? He's not going to meet Burke or go back to Sitka."

"Beats me. Wherever it is he's going, he's in one hell of a hurry." Hunter bellied back from the rim. "Keep your eyes open. With these boys running around like hornets, I want to make sure that horse is well hid."

She heard Hunter behind her and turned. He knelt in the shadow of the forest and motioned her impatiently to join him. Even before she reached him, she could read the excitement in his eyes.

"Over here, to the left," he told her, "you can see it good from there."

"See what, Mark, what is it?"

"Just wait," he grinned, "come on."

Jessie followed him through a thicket of vines along the edge of the ridge, twenty yards from where they'd watched the camp.

"There," Hunter pointed, "can you see it? Lean over and look down. I'll hold you."

Jessie went to her knees. There was no beach on this side of the ridge, only the water directly below. She saw the steamer at once. It was fifty yards offshore, chugging slowly around the point toward the camp. "It's—it's the boat that was after us, isn't it? The same one?"

"Sure it is." Mark grinned broadly. "See where they patched it up? The decking's still charred and so is the cabin. That's why Maksutova brought that cutter. I probably punched a hole in the steamer's boiler with my Sharps. Maksutova borrowed the cutter from someone in Sitka—or just took one he liked—and told the steamer's pilot to tag along behind. There are more men on board; I can't tell how many. Can't be more than a few."

"You're doing an awful lot of grinning," Jessie said narrowly. "What are you thinking about, Mark?"

"I'm thinking our ticket out of here just arrived."

119

Jessie stared. "You mean that?"

"Sure. Why not?"

"You don't think Maksutova's men will mind, huh?"

"I don't think we ought to ask. I think we ought to just do it."

Jessie had to grin. "Mr. Hunter, are you sure you're not from Texas? You've got the brag for it."

"All the really loco Texans come from *my* state," he said soberly. "Check around some time." He looked eagerly at the steamer. "I've got an idea how to do it. It ought to work, Jessie."

Jessie gave him a look. "Friend, it better be a whole lot better than *ought* to."

The high spur of rock over the gunmen's camp narrowed sharply to the south, away from the water. Jessie and Hunter led the horse to lower ground, keeping to the shelter of the trees. There was no sign of Maksutova's crew; they were searching the hills in earnest, but mostly to the south and to the west. They didn't imagine their quarry had bedded down at their own back door.

Hunter left her at the base of the rock wall and moved off quickly on foot to the south. Jessie took the horse and walked north. The dense curtain of trees ended abruptly and she could see the rocky beach and the squat little steamer. It was anchored ten yards offshore, bobbing gently in slate-gray water. She breathed a sigh of relief as she heard the low wheezing of the engine and saw the pale wisp of smoke from the rusty stack. If they'd shut down the engine, it was over. Starting from scratch and getting up steam was out of the question.

She watched the steamer a long time and decided there were two men aboard. One sat on the bow and made a smoke. The other moved around in the boxy cabin, then took a coil of line back to the stern. There were nine men in camp before the steamer pulled in with five more. Two were still aboard—twelve men she couldn't see and no way to tell how many were still in camp around the bend, how many were beating the bushes. There weren't enough horses for them all. And maybe all the men with horses weren't on the trail. Jessie shook her head and made a face. "Quit borrowing trouble," she told herself sternly. "You'll likely get all you can handle."

She heard the first shot off to the west. Seconds later, three more to the south. A man shouted, his voice alarmingly close. Horses crashed through brush far to the right. Moving back along the trail, she peered through branches toward the high ridge beyond. A thin column of smoke rose to the sky and drifted south. Jessie grinned. If the gunmen stopped to think, they'd know she and Hunter wouldn't give themselves away with a fire. Mark figured they wouldn't stop to work that one out—they'd still be thinking about the dead man hanging in a tree.

A blur of motion appeared through the trees. Jessie went to the ground and raised her rifle, then stood as she recognized Hunter. He was out of breath, his face flushed with heat.

"We got a bunch of 'em moving," he told her, "I don't know how many."

"We'll find out real soon," she said.

They ran back to the horse and looked at the steamer. The two men were standing atop the cabin shielding their eyes, trying to see what was up on shore. Jessie checked her Winchester. Hunter thumbed a .50 caliber shell into the big Sharps rifle. It was a powerful and deadly weapon, but not much use unless you could stop and reload—preferably out of range of other guns.

Hunter moved to the edge of the clearing while Jessie held the reins. Resting the barrel of the Sharps in the crook of a branch, he let out a breath and peered down the sights. The men atop the steamer were a good two hundred yards from his position. There would only be time to drop one. They'd have to get the other close up—before he had a chance to get them.

Jessie was ready for the shot, but the harsh, thunderous blast of the Big Fifty caused her to start. Smoke choked the clearing, and the sound rattled off the rocky walls. A man atop the steamer disappeared. His friend took cover at once. Hunter jammed the Sharps into its scabbard and threw his leg over the saddle. Almost before he was seated, Jessie was up behind him.

"All right," Hunter called out, "let's get her done." He kicked the mount hard, nearly throwing Jessie off. The horse tore out of the trees straight for the beach. Jessie bent low, one hand clutching Hunter's waist, the other grasping the Winchester rifle. The flat crack of a pistol came from the right. Jessie glanced back and saw a puff of blue smoke from the trees. Two men ran from the direction of the camp. One paused and blazed away with a rifle. Lead kicked gravel thirty yards to Jessie's right.

They were still a hundred yards from the water when the man on the steamer opened up. Hunter cursed and wrenched the horse sharply to the left. The mount protested, jerked its head, and nearly stumbled on rock. Jessie looked over her shoulder. There were still no riders in sight. The men on foot were running hard, snapping off shots on the move.

We'll make it—a little farther and we'll make it.

Hunter cried out and slapped his head. His hat flew off, and blood sprayed Jessie's cheek.

"Mark—Mark, you're hit!" she cried out.

Hunter didn't answer. He hunched low in the saddle, his chin pressed hard against his chest. Lead tugged at Jessie's jacket. Gray smoke flowered from the steamer. The man there was good or damn lucky.

"Hang on," Jessie shouted, "we'll make it, Mark! Mark, my God what are you doing!" The horse bolted crazily to the left. Hunter leaned dangerously in the saddle. Jessie stretched her hands under his arms and found the reins. "Let go," she shouted, "let go, I've got it!" Hunter slumped against her. Jessie gritted her teeth and jerked the mount hard to the right. The man on the steamer fired again. The shot whined inches from her head. Hunter nearly pushed her out of the saddle.

"All right," she said darkly, "to hell with this." She leaned back and brought the horse up short, slid out of the saddle, and tried to keep Hunter from falling. "Hold on," she snapped, "hold onto the horn and get down!"

Hunter groaned, let his leg slide over the saddle, and hung shakily to the horn.

"Stay there," Jessie told him. "Just hold on and keep going."

A bullet hit close, stinging her legs with gravel. Jessie went to her knees and squeezed off two shots at the steamer. Glass shattered and a head ducked quickly out of sight. She got a look at Hunter's face. Blood matted his hair and his flesh was drained of color. She bit her lip and fired another round at the steamer. The water was less than thirty yards away. She brought the reins over the horse's head and led it toward the shore, running as fast as Hunter would let her. A shout rose up from behind and she turned and saw the men coming toward her from the camp. Glancing warily back at the steamer, she kneeled again and let her sights drop over the man in the lead. The first shot missed. The second sent him sprawling, cursing and clutching at his leg.

"Jessie!" Hunter cried hoarsely.

Jessie whirled and sent a rapid volley of fire at the steamer. The man howled and dived for cover, came to his feet, and fired again. Jessie stood her ground, emptied the rifle, and saw the man slump to the deck. Lead geysered the water just ahead. Jessie jerked on the reins and cursed her horse. She paused ankle deep in the water, clawed in her jacket for shells, and levered three quickly into the chamber. Hunter hung on with one hand, leaned down, and splashed water in his face.

"You okay?"

"Yeah." He gave her a weak grin. "Tell you in a minute."

Jessie fired twice to slow her pursuers down, handed the rifle to Hunter, slapped the horse's rump. The animal protested, but moved in the water toward the steamer. Twenty feet from the ship, the bottom suddenly vanished. Jessie started swimming for the stern.

"Get around to the other side," she yelled out. "Get the ship between you and the beach!"

Lead punched a neat pattern of holes in the hull. Jessie gasped for air and joined Hunter. He was clinging to a line that hung in the water. The horse had paddled off. Jessie groaned to herself; the Sharps had gone with the mount.

"You're never going to get me up on that deck," Hunter said between his teeth. "Christ, Jessie."

"Fine. Just hang onto that line. I'll let you know when we

get to the Arctic Circle." She took the Winchester from him and tossed it onto the deck, then pulled herself over the low railing. Peering over the cabin, she saw three men working toward her through the water. She picked up the rifle and shot the closest man in the chest. The other two turned and splashed to shore. Jessie took a deep breath and calmly thumbed fresh shells into the rifle. She heard a sound behind her, whirled around, and brought her finger to the trigger.

"Shit, lady, don't!" The man she'd shot from shore was crawling toward her over the deck. He shut his eyes and made a face. "You already shot off my goddamn foot," he complained. "Ain't that enough?"

Jessie squinted at the man. He was small and wiry with a pinched weasel face. "Mister, you know how to run this thing?"

"Yeah, I can run it. Do it all the time."

"Then do it right now. Get us out of here fast."

"Can't. Takes about half an hour to get up steam."

Jessie pressed the cold circle against his head. "I've been on a steamboat before," she said tightly. "We've *got* steam, friend."

The man winced. "Hell, I can't even walk."

"Then *crawl*. Just do it!" She jammed the barrel against his nose. The man eased back on his hands, muttered between his teeth, and pulled himself forward. Jessie risked another look toward the shore. Her heart nearly stopped at the sight. Six men on horses were riding hard for the shore. With a sigh, she rested the rifle on the top of the cabin. At fifty yards she fired. A man spilled drunkenly out of the saddle. The other riders spread wide but kept coming. The engine rattled into life, violently shaking the decks. Jessie remembered something and moved toward the bow in a crouch. A small hand axe was mounted on the side of the cabin. She lifted it off its mount and moved into the open. A bullet splintered wood at her cheek. She hacked at the anchor rope until it parted, then dived for cover. The steamer moved lazily forward in the water. The riders on shore loosed a steady hail of bullets at the ship. Jessie moved back to the stern. Hunter had managed to get his chest and one arm on the deck. Jessie braced her legs on the railing and helped him up. Hunter sprawled on his back and gasped for air.

"We're moving," he said. "Who the hell's running this thing?"

"I don't know. You can ask him his name. Here." She handed him the axe. "Go down and see that he behaves. Can you make it all right?"

"I got any choice?"

Jessie grinned. "No, I don't guess you do." She left him and moved forward. Two riders were urging their mounts into the water. The others were fanned out along the shore, snapping off shots at the steamer. Jessie hit a horse in the rump and sent its rider tumbling into the water. Another gunman swore and emptied his Colt at the starboard bow. The steamer edged to port and slowly picked up speed. It suddenly occurred to Jessie that no one was at the wheel. She fired a few rounds to keep the gunmen honest, then crouched low and ducked into the cabin. When the boat was heading straight for open water, she sat down on the deck and waited for her hands to stop shaking.

★

Chapter 16

The land looked no different from the rugged, forested peaks they'd left on Chichagof Island. Still, Jessie felt a deep sense of relief, knowing they were passing the mainland of Alaska. Burke's men were now a good three hours behind; there was no way they could follow, unless Maksutova returned with the cutter. She knew, now, that wouldn't happen soon.

The man she'd shot was named Pete, and he didn't mind talking at all. He was glad he wasn't crippled or dead. He'd been on the steamer when Hunter had shot it up. Later, when the ship followed Maksutova's cutter to the northern camp, he'd heard what had happened to Ki and Natalia. If they were still alive, Maksutova was determined to find them. There was an Indian village to the east, in the shadow of the Chilkat Range. If Maksutova didn't find two bodies washed up somewhere, he'd go to the village and make the Tlingits help him search.

Jessie steadied herself on the deck, walked forward, and ducked into the shelter of the small cabin. Hunter sat in a chair bolted firmly to the deck, the Winchester resting on his knees. Pete glanced up from the wheel with no expression and turned back to his work. His foot wasn't exactly shot off as he'd imagined. Jessie had cut away his boot and bandaged the wound. Her bullet had plowed a quarter-inch furrow across his right heel. It was painful and would keep him limping for a while.

"You all right, Mark?" Jessie asked. "The head any better?"

"Can't tell if it's the head or the damn ocean making me dizzy," he said shortly.

Jessie checked the circle of cloth around his head and tried to loosen it a little. Hunter winced. The bullet had grazed his skull, leaving a sharp, throbbing pain in its wake. Hunter had told the man who'd shot him he'd better pray that he didn't pass out. If he even started to feel as if he might go under, he swore he'd shoot Pete in the head first.

Pete, Jessie decided, wasn't sure if he believed Hunter or not. She stepped up behind the man's high stool, bracing herself on the port bulkhead.

"How's the foot?" she asked. "Any time you want to lie down again, it's okay."

"Thanks," Pete muttered. He glanced sideways at Jessie. "Your friend don't like me much, miss. You tell him I ain't going to try anything, all right?"

"You just do what you're supposed to do," said Jessie.

"Now, I don't hold a thing 'gainst you for shooting me," he went on. "You understand what I'm saying? Hell, you just did what you had to do." He showed her an unconvincing grin. "I'm not a man that holds grudges."

"Well, Mr. Hunter there is," Jessie said flatly. "I'd remember that if I were you."

"Yeah, sure." Pete wet his lips. "I'll do that."

Jessie looked through the salt-encrusted window. It was the only piece of glass left on the steamer. Hunter had shot out most of the others off Baranof Island, and she'd taken care of the rest.

"We're not making any speed," Jessie told Pete. "Is this the best you can do? If I figured you were holding back, friend . . ."

"Lady, we're lucky we're making any way at all," Pete said

soberly. "Your friend back there damn near sunk us with that cannon of his. She's patched up eight ways to Sunday and I'm surprised if we're getting even six or seven knots."

"Six knots?" Hunter complained. "I can damn near walk faster than that!"

"You're sure welcome to try," Pete muttered.

"What was that?"

"Nothin'."

"That's not very fast," said Jessie. "How far is it to Yakutat Bay?"

"I never been there, but it's 'bout a 150 miles from where we started. We've come maybe twenty."

Jessie did some quick figuring in her head. "Lord, it'll take us maybe twenty-four hours!"

"Uh-huh," Pete said flatly, "it'll take at least that long. This isn't no Mississippi riverboat, lady. It's a little ol' sawed-off, forty-foot steamer. What's left of it. It's good enough for messin' around the coast, but it's not going to take you to the Sandwich Islands or the Japans."

"Yakutat Bay will be just fine," Jessie said coolly.

"Yeah, well, it'll get us there. But not as fast as you'd like," Pete told her. "Even if we could make full steam there's the question of wood. You saw how much we had and what's left. We're going to have to stop and get more."

"Like hell we are," Hunter said darkly.

"I'm afraid he's right," Jessie sighed. "We are burning up fuel, Mark."

Pete showed her a nasty grin. "You don't mind me saying so, miss, you could go back and stoke a little more if you've a mind to. That needle's dropping fast. I'd do it myself, 'cept I got this hole you put in my foot."

Jessie ignored the remark. "And how are we going to get this wood, chop it?"

"Don't have to do that. There's a couple half-breeds run a wood camp up the coast. Thirty, maybe thirty-five miles. Right in the shadow of Mt. Fairweather."

"I thought you'd never been this way before," Hunter said narrowly.

128

"I said I'd never been as far as Yakutat, mister. Yakutat's north of that. The wood camp's maybe halfway."

Jessie looked at Hunter. "From there, it's maybe seventy-five miles to where we're going."

"About that."

Pete gave Jessie a curious look. "None of my business, of course, but what do you folks expect to do when you get there? I got no idea why Mr. Burke hightailed it up north, but I know how many men he's got with him."

"You're right," Jessie said evenly, "it's none of your business. Just get us there, friend."

Jessie guessed it was well after eight in the evening when they spotted the dim yellow lights on shore.

"That's them," Pete told her, "that's the half-breeds' place. Three lanterns in a line."

Hunter stood and walked shakily to the wheel next to Pete. "You ever been in there at night? How about rocks or shallow water?"

Pete gave him a pained look. "Wouldn't make no difference if I hadn't, now would it? We aren't goin' another ten miles on what we got back there in the pile."

"Anything happens," Jessie said, "he gets drowned the same as we do, Mark."

"Yeah, well," Hunter said grudgingly, "maybe you can steer this thing as good as you can shoot."

Pete beamed, surprised and pleased at the unexpected compliment. "You know where it was I learned to shoot?"

"No, where?"

"I rode with Jesse James for two years. Would've been with him and Frank and the Youngers on that Northfield raid, 'cept I was laid up bad with influenza. Damn near died. Course that was better'n what happened to the fellers that did get to go." He squinted at Hunter in the dark. "What do you think about that?"

"I think you're lying through your teeth," Hunter told him.

Pete gave him a sheepish grin. "Learned to shoot on the Missouri is what happened. Worked on a riverboat taking stuff

129

up to the army at Fort Benton. Got good enough with a rifle so they'd let me hunt game instead of work."

"Then why did you tell me all that shit about the James Boys?"

Pete gave an easy shrug. "Sounds a lot more interestin' than chasing deer and rabbits." He turned back to the wheel, fighting a strong northerly wind that threatened to push the ship out to sea. The steep wooded shore loomed above, blotting out the sky. Jessie decided the man knew what he was doing; in spite of the wind and offshore currents, he guided the steamer easily past the three yellow lanterns into the shelter of a glacier-carved fiord. The inlet was steep and rocky on three sides. To the left, the forest sloped down to the shore. A lantern hung at the end of the dock. Cords of wood were stacked neatly on the landing. Jessie could make out a cabin back in the trees. A man walked out on the dock, stood under the lantern, and watched them approach.

"You know these fellas, do you?" asked Hunter.

"Sure I do. Told you that. I been here three or four times."

"Just be real careful what you say," Hunter warned him. He shoved the rifle hard under Pete's right ear. "The thing is, Pete, if it happened to turn out these half-breeds of yours worked for Kodiak Burke, you're going to wish you'd tried to rob that Northfield bank."

Pete snorted. "Mister, these ol' boys don't give a damn who buys their wood. Just so you got the money to pay." He turned the wheel to starboard and cut the engine. The sudden silence seemed deafening after the long hours at sea.

"Someone's got to hail 'em," Pete said. "You want to do it or you want me to?"

"You do it," Jessie put in. "And like Mr. Hunter says, don't try anything cute."

"Hello the shore," Pete called out. "It's Pete Bleeker on the *Sitka Star.*"

The man on the dock laughed deeply in his chest. "Hell, I know who it is. Ain't another tub dirtier than that one on the coast. I smelled you coming this morning."

"Just sell me some damn wood," Pete grumbled. "I didn't

come for no talk." He turned to Jessie and Hunter. "One of you get those lines—I'm not fit to walk."

"I'll do it," said Hunter. He handed the rifle to Jessie and ducked outside the cabin. In a moment, the steamer bumped gently against the dock. The wooden columns were wrapped heavily with sacking and rope. Hunter returned and looked at Pete. "Don't do any talking you don't have to," he warned. "Tell this fella we're Will and Mary Woods if he asks."

Pete nodded. "You going to keep on pokin' that rifle in my back, he's going to get some curious about that."

"Don't you worry," Jessie told him, "we'll handle it." She pulled the little derringer from behind her buckle, showed it to Pete, and jammed it in his ribs. "Just behave yourself, mister."

"You folks are full of tricks, ain't you?" Pete grumbled. He looked at Hunter. "You going to lend me a hand, or am I supposed to crawl out of here?"

Hunter muttered under his breath and draped Pete's arm over his shoulder, clutching the Winchester in his free hand. Jessie followed, keeping the derringer close to Pete's back. The man on the dock leaned down to help. He let his eyes roam boldly over Jessie's figure and glanced curiously at Pete's foot and the bandage on Hunter's head.

"What the hell happened to you folks," he grinned. "You rassle a bear or what?"

"Ran into rough weather," Hunter muttered.

"Damned if you didn't." He was a heavyset, barrel-chested man with a thick black beard and long hair. "Come up to the cabin and get yourself some hot coffee and eats," he said. "We'll get you loaded up. Billy," he called over his shoulder, "get your ass on down here!"

Another man appeared at the end of the dock and walked toward them. Jessie's eyes darted to Hunter.

"Thanks for the hospitality," Hunter said. "We need to get going as soon as we can."

"Suit yourself." The big man closed one eye and shrugged. The man named Billy looked over the newcomers and started stacking wood at the end of the dock. The bearded man turned away to help, bent down, and came up fast, moving on the balls of his feet.

"Mark!" Jessie shouted a warning.

Hunter threw Pete at the bearded man and backed off, bringing his rifle to bear on the other's belly. The man swung a short length of wood in his fist and knocked the barrel aside. The rifle slid away along the dock. The bearded man lowered his head like a bull and rammed his shoulder in Hunter's chest. The man named Billy went for Jessie. The derringer exploded twice. Billy screamed and clawed at his face. Jessie went for the rifle—the bearded man saw her, came at her, and clubbed her to the ground. Jessie hit hard, gasped, and came to her knees. The side of her face was numb. The bearded man stood above her and grinned.

"Goddamn if you ain't pretty," he said. "Hell of a lot better'n them Tlingit squaws. Billy—quit your cryin' and git up!"

"She ruint my face, Ham," Billy whined. "Shit, it hurts bad!"

Jessie glanced at Hunter. He lay on his back unmoving. Pete leaned against the woodpile and watched. Ham squatted down and brought his face close to Jessie's. Jessie cringed at his foul breath. Ham laughed, reached down, and ripped her shirt to her waist. Jessie cried out as his rough hands clutched her breasts.

"My Gawd," Ham breathed, his dark eyes alive with hunger, "this night's sure turning out some better'n I figured."

Light from the main room of the cabin cast a narrow band of yellow under the door. Jessie could see the shadows of the men's feet as they moved about, hear the rattle of tin cups, Ham's drunken bellow and Billy's high-pitched laughter. Once, Ham lurched against a table and fell. He cursed and threw a bottle at the wall.

Hunter let a sharp breath pass between his teeth. He struggled against his ropes and looked at the door. "Damn it, Jessie, we should've known better—that lyin' little son of a bitch never told the truth in his life!"

"We knew there might be trouble," Jessie said evenly. "We

had no choice, Mark. There was no way to go any farther with the steamer. Pete wasn't lying about that."

"I'm glad he told the truth about something," Hunter said darkly. "I sure feel a hell of a lot better."

Jessie stretched as far as she could. Craning her neck she could make out his face in the dim light. There was an ugly bruise on his jaw. If Ham had hit him in the head, she was certain the blow would have killed him.

"Are you all right? How does your head feel now?"

"No better than it ought to."

"Mark, I've tried to do something with these ropes. I don't think anything's going to work."

Hunter didn't answer. Jessie glanced around the small room. It was a shed, built onto the back of the cabin to hold supplies. There were ropes and cans of paint, sacks of potatoes and onions on the dirt floor, and sides of venison and ham hung overhead. The cold ground chilled her to the bone. Ham had torn her shirt completely away and left her bare to the waist.

"Jessie," Hunter said beside her, "when they come they're going to let you loose for a minute, probably take you out front. If they—if they cut you free right here try to push one of 'em to me. I can still kick, and maybe you can make a run for it."

Jessie shrank back as the door jerked open. Ham's big frame was a shadow against the light.

"You ready for me, lady?" His words came out in a slur. "I'm sure as hell ready for you!" He reached down and pulled her roughly to her feet. Jessie saw it, then, over his shoulder, a quick glimpse and it was gone. Her skin crawled and a scream stuck in her throat. They had cleared a big plank table in the other room. Short strands of wire were tied to the four corners and Jessie knew with sudden horror what they were for.

"Get her legs, Billy," Ham grinned. "I'll take the other end. Gawd, just look at them tits! Pete—put a bullet in that son of a bitch."

"No!" Jessie cried.

"Be my pleasure," Pete said darkly.

Jessie saw Pete lean against the door on his makeshift crutch, saw his hand slide to the Colt in his belt. She flailed out,

133

kicking against her bonds. Ham and Billy carried her struggling out of the shed. Pete laughed behind her and she heard the single explosion of the pistol, the sound so loud in the small cabin she was certain it would go on forever.

Chapter 17

"Oh, God. *No!*" Jessie screamed in horror and disbelief. Ham gripped her arms and slammed her hard against the table. She felt the wire loops twist painfully around her wrists.

"You didn't have to kill him," she said hoarsely "You didn't have to murder him, you son of a bitch!"

Ham grinned. "Lady, once you been pleasured by ol' Ham here you ain't even going to remember that poor bastard. Ain't that right now, Billy?"

Jessie's fear turned to rage. She jerked her feet from Billy's grip and slammed her boot hard into the man's belly. Billy gasped and went sprawling. Ham threw back his head and bellowed with delight. Billy came to his feet, one watery eye glazed with anger.

For the first time, Jessie clearly saw his ruined face, the half-closed eye and the bruised flesh, the black grains of powder in his cheek where her derringer had exploded. Billy reached for her legs and Jessie flailed out and tried to kick him again. Billy gave her feet a wide berth and slapped her hard across the face. Jessie cried out as tears blurred her eyes. Billy climbed awkwardly up on the table and straddled her legs.

"You owe me plenty," he said dully, "and I sure aim to collect, woman. You just see if I don't!"

Jessie forced a laugh. "You ever have a woman wasn't tied down, Billy? Hell, you ever have one at all?" Billy hit her again. Jessie moaned and tasted blood.

"You keep that up you goin' to rile that boy bad," Ham said solemnly.

Billy worked at the buckle of her belt. Jessie closed her eyes and shrank from his touch. Ham chuckled deep in his chest and moved down to grip her legs, while Billy slid off the table and peeled her denims past her ankles.

"Damn, lookee there," Ham said in wonder. "Billy, we goin' to make this one last a long time."

"Three or four days," Billy nodded. "Hell, a week—I want her a whole week, Ham!"

Jessie shuddered as the cold strands of wire pressed her ankles to the table. Billy's hands explored her naked body. Jessie felt bile rise to her throat. Ham grinned as he peeled out of his trousers. Billy's jaw fell as his hands moved up between Jessie's legs. She heard Pete's crutch scrape the floor, glanced up, and saw his arm stretched straight out from his shoulder, the .45 clutched in his hand. Billy blinked and opened his mouth and Pete shot him in the face. Ham straightened, his trousers at his knees, and Pete pulled the trigger three times. Jamming the weapon in his belt, he hobbled to the end of the table and freed Jessie's legs, then moved up to loosen her hands.

"Your man's all right," he said evenly, "I didn't shoot him. You'd best go get him loose."

"Pete—"

"There's things a man can stomach and things he can't," Pete said. "I never did nothin' like this, and I guess I don't figure on startin'." He let his eyes dart once over Jessie's naked flesh, then scowled down at the floor. "I'll be outside. I need to get me some air."

When Jessie and Hunter left the cabin, Pete had a bridle and a blanket on a horse and was struggling with the saddle. Hunter

136

took it from him and finished the job. Pete nodded and leaned against the cabin to fix a smoke.

"I'm headed up to the Yukon or maybe back south," he told Jessie. "Anywhere there ain't salt water. I 'bout had enough of that. There's horses here if you want 'em, or you got yourself the *Sitka Star*. I sure as hell don't figure on boarding her again."

"Thank you, Pete," Jessie said gently. "We're grateful for what you did."

Pete shrugged off her thanks. He glanced cautiously at Hunter. "No hard feelings either way. That okay with you?"

"We're evened up," Hunter told him.

Pete grinned wearily at the pair. "Real peculiar how things'll turn out, now ain't it?" Past him, the first dull hint of morning touched the mountains. "I never liked them two. Ham and that Billy. Never liked 'em at all."

By late afternoon, the heights of Mt. Fairweather were shrouded in clouds far aft of the steamer's wake. Hunter decided it was a good ninety miles from the woodcamp to Yakutat Bay. At the steamer's snaillike pace, they'd be lucky to make it by dawn the next morning.

"It better be sometime before sunup," Jessie reminded him. "I don't figure on running into Kodiak Burke in broad daylight. Not chugging along in this."

Hunter steadied the wheel, keeping the ship's bow pointed steadily northwest. The tree-lined shore was only a hundred yards to starboard. He turned soberly and faced Jessie.

"And when we get there. Then what? You given any thought to that?"

"Of course, I have. I haven't thought of much else, Mark."

"And?"

"And I don't have the slightest idea," she said. Her green eyes looked steadily into his. "How are we going to stop Kodiak Burke—just the two of us? Is that what you want to know?"

Hunter showed her a painful grin. "Dumb question, huh?"

"Yes. Dumb question. And I don't pretend to have the answer. We'll do whatever we can. Damn it, Mark, it's crazy. You don't have to tell me that!"

She stood abruptly and pulled her jacket about her shoulders.

He was watching her intently. She met his eyes, understanding what she saw there at once. She had seen it before and let it go unanswered. Now, she held out her hands and let him draw her into the circle of his arms. When her lips met his, a shudder of excitement swept through her body. Hunter groaned and pressed himself against her. The taste of his mouth sent a fiery surge of desire to her belly and the tips of her breasts. His hands gripped her shoulders, slid to the narrow curve of her waist. Jessie sighed and pushed him away.

"This is a fine time for us to start figuring out what we should've figured last night," she said wryly. "Who do you suppose is going to man this tub while we're off doing somethin' else?"

"I was afraid you'd think of that," Hunter scowled. "And I did think of it last night, by the way."

"You did? I sure didn't notice."

"I wasn't sure it was the right time. You were worried about Ki, whether he'd gotten away or not."

Jessie smiled and touched his cheek. "Thank you, Mark. I was worried about Ki. I still am. But I wanted you last night all the same, just like I do right now. Damn it all, we've sure got awful timing, don't we?"

Hunter gripped her shoulders and made a face. "You're not going to believe this. I miss Pete. If he were here, he could steer this thing, and we could go back aft."

Jessie laughed. "Love in the boiler room. Sounds scandalous, Mark."

"Sounds pretty good to me." Hunter kissed her soundly and turned to correct their course.

Jessie paused, frowned, and bit her lip. She had pressed her right hand along the left sleeve of her fleece-lined jacket, gripped it hard with her fingers. There was something there, something that didn't belong. Maybe the fleece was coming apart, slipping down her sleeve. She peeled off the jacket and stuck her hand in the sleeve. There was a small tear in the lining. Her fingers touched something slick and she pulled it free. It was a narrow oilskin packet, the size and shape of an envelope, sealed tightly with wax.

Mark gave her a puzzled look. "What's that?"

"I don't know." Jessie frowned. "I don't know what it is or what it's doing in my jacket." She moved to a bench at the rear of the small cabin, turned up the wick on the lamp, and opened the package. There was a sheaf of folded papers inside. A chill touched the back of her neck at the sight of the familiar, spidery script.

"Mark," she said, drawing in a breath, "Mark, it's from Platte—this is Hiram Platte's writing!"

"What? Then how did it—"

"The Indian!" Jessie exclaimed. "The man at Burke's house, the one Maksutova murdered in my room at the hotel. This is what he was trying to get to me, Mark. Maksutova's men surprised him in my room and he hid this packet in the first place he could find. He stuffed it in the lining of my jacket, and when Ki went back to the hotel he brought the jacket to me. My God, Mark!" She bent low to the light and began to read.

It was all there, everything Platte had learned about Kodiak Burke and the cartel's Alaskan operations. Names, places, men Burke had murdered, and companies he had stolen.

"This plot your man talks of, the people he calls the Europeans—I knew Burke was mixed up with something big; I just didn't know what." He studied her thoughtfully a long moment. "You do, though, don't you? You know exactly what he's talking about."

"Yes, I do, Mark. I had a good idea who Burke was before I ever got to Alaska."

She told him, then, the story of her father's fight against the Prussian cartel, the fight she and Ki had taken on at her father's death. She told him what the cartel had done, the power they sought to gain, and the part Kodiak Burke played in their plans for Alaska. When she was finished, Hunter stared for a long time into the growing dark.

"Lady," he said finally, "you've got your hand in the biggest barrel of alligators I ever saw."

"I know," she said dryly, "and once you stick your hand in that barrel, it's hard to take it out without losin' a couple of fingers. Or an arm or a leg."

"Looks to me like you've got all your parts in the right places."

Jessie showed him a weary smile and clasped his hand. "You would think of that, now wouldn't you? Mark, there's something else here. On these last two sheets. Hiram Platte was trying to put down all his thoughts, things he figured I ought to know. I'm sure he wrote all this not long before Burke had him murdered. This last part, though . . ." Jessie shook her head and met Hunter's eyes. "Mark, remember the Aleut who told Nikolai Shelikhov about the wreck of the *Okhotsk?* Platte knew him—he knew him and he helped him get out of Sitka."

"What?" Mark frowned and Jessie handed him the papers. Hunter scanned them quickly, then read aloud:

> " . . . *the man came to me through some of the Tlingits of my acquaintance in Sitka. I speak very little of the Aleut tongue, but enough to know that he was terribly frightened. This is the reason the Tlingits brought him to me. They trust me and know that I will do my best to see him safely away. He would not say why he came to Sitka, but it was clear that he feared for his life. I allowed him to hide in my loft until the Tlingits could take him by canoe up the coast.*
>
> "*I cannot imagine what this old man is doing so far from his home in the north. One thing though is certain. From his gestures, I know who it is that he fears. It can be no other than that devil Maksutova. Why Burke's man is after this poor Indian I cannot say. When he left me, I went to the loft where he had stayed and found something most peculiar there. He had found a piece of charcoal and nearly covered the walls with some marking. I reproduce that marking here.*
>
> "*It appears to be a crude, broken cross,*

*but I know for a fact that this man is no
Christian. I suspect, as I did upon first meeting him, that his mind had succumbed some-
what to the infirmity of age. Whoever he may
be, I had the pleasure and satisfaction of
seeing him safely away, free Maksutova's
grasp . . ."*

Hunter shrugged and passed the paper back to Jessie. "I
don't know. It doesn't make any sense."

"It didn't make any sense to Platte, either. But he knew the
Aleut was mixed up with Maksutova somehow—and Maksutova meant Kodiak Burke." Jessie sighed. "He was right,
too; he just never knew it. It's plain enough from what he wrote
here that the old man didn't tell him a thing about going to see
Shelikhov."

Jessie stood and stared into the dark, thinking of Hiram
Platte. He must have known that Burke would kill him, that it
was only a matter of time. Yet, he meticulously set to paper
the things he knew, hoping the information would somehow
reach her. Anger welled up to constrict her throat. *Damn them,
damn them all!* she cried out silently. How many men like
Platte would have to die before it was over, before the faceless
men of the cartel were silenced forever? Would it happen?
Could it?

It has to—it has to be—she answered herself.

Hunter added wood to the wheezing engine, and Jessie stood
watch at the wheel while he slept. Sometime after ten, fog
began to roll in from the Pacific. Jessie watched her compass
heading, praying she wasn't steering them out to sea or veering
straight into the rocky shore. By midnight, the fog was so thick
it crept into the cabin itself. Jessie started to wake Hunter, but
knew he could do no more than she was doing herself.

The ship's clock said twenty after two in the morning. Hunter
groaned in his sleep, and Jessie turned to see if he was all
right. If the fog hadn't parted, if her eyes hadn't darted in the
right direction at that instant, she would have missed it. She

141

stood where she was, gripping the wheel, unable to move, unable to draw a breath. The cutter slipped past her like a ghost, not fifty feet to port, appearing and vanishing in an instant, its heading the same as the small cutter. She only saw it for a second and it was gone, but she knew with a terrible certainty when and where she had seen it before.

Ki could hear them now, tearing through the brush, sweeping the branches aside. They were Maksutova's crew, white men, making too much noise to be Indians. He looked at Natalia and saw the fine sheen of moisture on her face, saw the glacier-blue eyes wide with fear, a mindless animal fear she couldn't control. "Go," he told her, "run, Natalia. I'll catch up, I'll be there." She knew he was lying, that if she turned away she'd never see him again. A cry stuck in her throat and she ran into his arms. Ki pushed her roughly away and slapped her hard across the face. "Go, damn you," he said harshly. "Go, get out of here!" She turned, then, and ran, a hurt and uncomprehending look in her eyes.

He stopped the first one, coming up off the ground and driving the blade in the man's belly and pulling him silently off the path and into the brush with a single motion. Blood flecked a stand of lacy ferns. He stopped the second man and then the third with his bare hands. The fourth came up the path too soon, sounding the alarm and bringing the others on the run.

He knew they had Natalia. Maksutova had come down to tell him that. Through his pain, Ki remembered what the giant Russian had told him about the girl. They were things that he wanted to forget.

He knew a night and a day had passed on the ship. Maybe more than that. Time had a single meaning now. Time was the interval between his visits from Maksutova. There was a time of pain and a time when pain subsided. The Russian knew all about pain. He knew there was a time when a man couldn't feel it anymore. There was no use hurting until the flesh and the bone and the nerves could know exactly what was happening

142

to them again. There was a time when the body was so sensitive to the hurt that had come before, when feeling was coming back with all its fury, that even the slightest touch was a horror. Maksutova knew exactly when this moment would come again. When it did, he would open the hold and climb down the ladder, and for an instant Ki would know whether daylight or darkness touched the world. An instant after that, he didn't care.

The early morning air hurt his skin. The unfamiliar light of the lanterns seared his eyes. He was dimly aware that they had hauled him up the ladder on a rope. The pain had put him under at once and he was grateful.

When he awoke once more, Ki thought that death had claimed him. He was floating in air. The cool, moist wind smelled good. Clean white clouds wreathed his body. Soon, perhaps, he would meet his samurai master. He had many things to tell the old man. He was looking forward to that.

"Hirata Sensei, I am here . . . you must help me, for I know nothing of the afterworld!"

Ki waited, but no one answered.

A moment later the pain returned. Ki screamed. It was as much a cry of anger as of pain. Clearly, he wasn't dead yet. Nothing seemed to be working out right.

★

Chapter 18

The fog hung thick and heavy about the steamer through the early morning hours. At first light, a crisp westerly breeze began to drive the gray wall toward the land. Jessie was on deck and saw it first—a small rent in the mist off the starboard revealing a patch of gray-green water. The rent widened and let a hazy shadow appear.

Jessie stared and grasped the railing. Hunter heard her and joined her and saw it, too.

"Great God A'mighty," he muttered under his breath.

There it was, suddenly visible out of the mist, the rocky shore and the tree-lined slope behind it, and towering over that, the most awesome sight either of the two had ever imagined. It was a wall—a sheer white wall of solid ice looming three hundred feet into the lightening sky. There was a hint of the massive body of the glacier beyond, the great sheet of ice stretching back into the haze of the mountains. Now, though, the mouth of the monster itself was all their eyes could handle, the great jagged teeth clamped shut upon the earth.

"We found it," Hunter said, keeping his voice low as if his words might start the wall grinding south again. "It's Malaspina, Jessie—we're either right in Yakutat Bay or still on the Pacific side of the glacier. If that compass is still working, I'd say we're in the bay. The glacier's due west. If we were still seaward, it'd be to our north."

"If you're right," Jessie said evenly, "we'd better get ourselves ashore. If that fog burns off and we're floating out here like a duck..."

"Right," Hunter agreed, guessing her thoughts at once. He hadn't seen the ghostly spectre of the cutter, passing swiftly in the night, but Jessie had described it all too well.

They anchored the steamer behind a narrow hook of land, well hidden from the water. Jessie saw she needn't have worried about the fog. They were halfway to shore when the sky turned black and a hard driving rain blew in from the west.

"Now where the hell did that come from?" Hunter growled. Water streamed down his face, and his clothes were plastered to his skin.

"Quit complaining," said Jessie. "If that cutter's close by, you can bet everyone'll be down below. We made it, Mark. And no one knows we're here. That's about all the advantage we've got."

"We've got an advantage and a problem," Hunter said thoughtfully. "They won't likely find us if we're careful. On the other hand, we're going to have a hell of a time figuring where they are, so we can stay out of their way. As for finding that wreck..." Hunter shook his head. "I told you that ice sheet covers maybe a thousand or fifteen hundred square miles. Yakutat Bay's, say, twenty miles wide and forty miles deep. Hell, something like that. I wish I had a chart."

"I get the picture," Jessie told him. She listened to the deafening roar of the rain on the roof of the *Sitka Star*. They were sitting on a pile of worn blankets in the boiler room; the engine was quiet now, but Hunter had opened the fire door to let in some heat. Jessie sighed and leaned against his shoulder. The glow around the edge of the door cast warm shadows across the small room. She could almost believe they were somewhere else—a cabin in the mountains, a camp in some sheltered canyon, safe from harm.

Hunter moved closer and slipped his arm tightly about her. "You're shaking," he said. "You still cold?"

"Yes, some. And I guess I'd be lying if I said I wasn't a little scared, too."

"If you weren't, I'd say you didn't have a lick of sense."

Jessie turned her head to face him, and Hunter touched her cheek and drew her to him. She gave a little cry and buried her head against his chest. All the fear and pain buried within her suddenly burst through at once. Hunter's touch brushed the corners of her eyes and found the softness of her mouth. Jessie sighed and opened her lips to his caresses. The rain lashed relentlessly on the roof of the vessel. Jessie watched a vein pulse rapidly in Hunter's throat. His muscles tensed, growing hard as iron. She slid her hands about his shoulders and pressed herself against him, savoring the taste of his kisses. The hard, pulsing thrust of his tongue explored every corner of her mouth, teasing each secret hollow of delight. Jessie let the pink tip of her tongue flick past his lips, matching his hunger with her own. His kisses seemed to smolder in her belly, burn the tips of her breasts.

Hunter moaned deeply within his chest, letting his mouth trail down her throat to the firm swell of her breasts. Jessie's pulse quickened at his touch. She gazed at him, a soft and lazy smile on her lips. Hunter's eyes met hers, but neither spoke. Both sensed this was not a time for words. Releasing her grip about his shoulder, she brought her hands to her shirt and shakily opened the buttons. Hunter drew in a breath at the sight, the delicate curve of her breasts, the hard points of her nipples. His hands found the buckle of her belt; his fingers worked impatiently at the buttons of her tight denim pants. He slid his fingers beneath the cloth, and Jessie raised her legs to let him peel the denims down past her ankles.

"My God, Jessie . . ." Hunter gazed at her body with open wonder. "I wanted this to happen the minute I saw you."

Jessie grinned. "So did I—when I got off the boat and picked your face out of the crowd." She reached up to touch his cheek. "I changed my mind real quick when I thought you worked for Kodiak Burke. I'm sure glad I was wrong, Mark."

Hunter didn't answer. He stood quickly and tugged the wet shirt out of his trousers, loosed the buttons, and cast the garment aside. Bending to wrench off his boots, he slid his trousers down his hips and kicked them free.

Jessie absently ran the tip of her tongue across her lips. The sight of his naked body sent a deep surge of excitement through her veins. He was lean and hard-bodied; cords of muscle banded his frame from his shoulders to the flat plane of his belly. Dark hair covered his chest. She gazed in awe at his erection; the rigid spear of his manhood stood only inches from her face.

"Lord, you are worth waitin' for, mister!" she sighed. "Is that all for me, Mark?"

"No one else," Hunter whispered. He grasped the slim circle of her waist and brought her to him.

"Yes, *yes!*" Jessie cried. She arched her back off the floor, twisting in a sensuous curve beneath his touch. The motion hollowed her belly and thrust her breasts up to meet him. Hunter brought his lips to the firm swell of her flesh. With the tip of his tongue he traced the dusky shadow circling her breast. The path of his touch grew ever smaller until he moistened the dimpled flesh and caressed her nipples.

Jessie's breath came faster. Her breasts rose under his touch, thrusting eagerly against his lips. Hunter's mouth drew the rosy peaks past his teeth. His kisses raced like fire through her body. He teased her taut nipples, flipping the pert buds until each small touch made her shudder. Hunter's lips left her breasts and trailed down the hollow between her ribs to the gentle swell of her belly. Jessie gave a quick cry of joy, relishing the thrill of what was coming. She gripped the floor and thrust her belly boldly up to meet him. His hands found the soft curve of her back, the plush globes of her bottom. His mouth brushed the feathery edge of her treasure; the heat of his breath was a brand against her thighs. He lingered over the velvet flesh of her belly, traced a thin line down her navel to the silken mound below.

147

When he kissed the creamy hollows of her thighs, Jessie gave a lazy little sigh. Gently, he touched her sensitive flesh, exploring delicate folds. Jessie opened her mouth, lips stretched tight against her teeth. Hunter kissed the sweet flesh, carefully avoiding the point where she wanted him most. He taunted the honeyed nest, his lips moving closer and closer to the crown. Jessie felt the fires of release burning within her. Her nails clawed at the deck. Her body arched off the floor on the slim columns of her legs.

"Take me," she begged him. "Take me, Mark, please!"

Hunter marveled at the beauty before his eyes. The lovely sight quickened his pulse and hardened his rigid member even further. His lips brushed the slick coral flesh; his tongue slid gently over her, glistening with the heat of passion. She writhed uncontrollably under his touch.

Suddenly, Hunter thrust his tongue. A ragged cry escaped her lips. Hunter probed again and again, tasting the spice of her flesh. Jessie felt the warmth within her glow. It flowed like a hot and sugary syrup from her belly to the rigid points of her nipples. Rivulets of moisture streaked the hollow of her belly. Hunter's lips closed gently. Jessie screamed and bit her lip, bringing the coppery taste of blood. The power of her release wrenched every fiber of her being. One wave of pleasure after another lifted her up and tossed her aside, each spasm stronger than the last. She exploded again and again, letting the hungry fires consume her. One final, agonizing burst of pain and pleasure surged through her thighs, and she fell back limply to the ground.

"Oh, Lord," she sighed, "I don't think I've ever been loved so good!"

"I'm sure sorry to hear that," Mark said soberly.

"What?" Jessie looked puzzled.

"I was kinda hoping the next part would be the best."

"What next part are you—Mark, Mark what are you doing!"

Hunter laughed, edged his hands beneath her hips and flipped her roughly onto her belly. Jessie squealed and kicked her long legs in the air. Hunter set her down on her knees and crawled quickly between her thighs. Jessie spread her legs and twisted her bottom in a delightful invitation. Hunter teased her relentlessly, letting his hands caress her thighs and brush the supple flesh between her legs.

"Mark, I can't stand it," Jessie pleaded.

"Can't stand what? More loving, or waiting for more?"

"Both, damn you," she said crossly. "I'm—I'm so pleasured out now I'm 'bout to fall right on my face, but if you don't do something soon I'm going to scream."

Hunter grinned. "No big hurry as I see it. This rain's likely to keep up forever. We can just laze around awhile till you get back your strength. Wouldn't want to strain you."

"Mark Hunter," Jessie fumed, "you're driving me crazy. If you don't—aaaaah, yes!"

Suddenly, Hunter eased her thighs still farther apart and rammed his shaft deep inside her. Jessie cried out and gasped for breath. Hunter gripped her slender waist and thrust himself against her in long, rapid strokes. He drew her to him with his hands, pushed her back, then drew her to him again. Jessie matched his rhythm with her own. Her body filled with his warmth, bringing her ever closer to the delicious flood that would carry her away. It was there, ready to take her over the edge.

Hunter groaned and went rigid, slammed himself against her in a final, fiery thrust. Jessie's head snapped rapidly from side to side, lashing copper hair across her back. Liquid heat licked at her loins and Hunter released himself. Jessie opened her mouth in a long, silent scream and let her orgasm consume her. Hunter sighed above her as she fell on her belly and gasped for air. He came down beside her, gently turned her on her back, and took her in his arms.

"You all right?" he whispered.

"I will be—in about three or four weeks. Lord, Mark, that was some fine loving!"

"Yeah. I kinda recall that it was."

"You do, huh?" Jessie raised a wary brow. "Sure glad you noticed."

"I notice a lot of things."

"Like what?"

149

"It's stopped raining."

Jessie raised her head and listened. "You're right." She gave him an impish grin. "Wonder why I didn't notice that?"

Hunter held her cheeks within his hands and kissed her soundly. "I know why I didn't notice. I can only handle one good storm at a time."

Jessie laughed. "Is that what I am? A good storm?"

"Lady, you are a summer's worth of thunder and lightning—and a little of next spring thrown in."

Jessie snuggled warmly into the curve of his shoulder. "I like it," she said smugly. She kissed the hard muscle of his arm. "Don't think I've ever been anyone's storm before."

Hunter raised up on his arms and touched the tip of his finger to her still rigid nipple. "Can I ask a question?"

"Well, sure."

"How would you feel about bein' one again?"

The fog swept in once more to replace the rain. The sun was shining somewhere above a thin layer of clouds, tinting the fog with an eerie, luminous glow. Jessie and Hunter walked through a ghostly forest along the shore. The glacier was at their backs, less than a mile to the west, hidden under a dense blanket of mist. They couldn't see it, but they could feel its icy breath, sense its awesome presence.

They had left the steamer at noon, moving northeast and climbing the tree-lined slope. Hunter thought if they could gain a little height they might get their bearings when the fog finally vanished.

"We're either somewhere on the Pacific coast," Hunter said sourly, "or inside Yakutat Bay. Either that, or we're somewhere else."

"Come on," Jessie chided, "what do you mean somewhere else? The glacier's here; we can't be far off."

"Jessie," he said solemnly, "we came up the coast in the fog. We don't have more than a guess how far we went. We could have passed Malaspina and gone—hell, I don't know, quite a few miles farther than we thought."

"What are you trying to say?"

"That there's more than one glacier up this coast past Yakutat Bay. I wouldn't know one from the other."

"My God," Jessie breathed, "I'm glad you didn't tell me this before."

"I didn't want to tell you now. Figured I ought to say something just in case. I think we're all right, Jessie. I'm next to certain we are."

"My God . . ."

"You just said that."

"Well I'm saying it again, all right?"

They kept moving northeast up the slope. Jessie guessed they'd been gone from the steamer a good four, five hours. It was late in the afternoon. If they didn't start back soon they'd have to try to find the ship in the dark. And then what? Start over in the morning? Hope they were in the right bay and not somewhere else?

The trees ended abruptly at a steep river of rock. Sometime in the past, the whole side of the ridge had given way, taking a mile-long section of the forest down with it. The fog was thinning now, and Jessie and Hunter could see the bay below, its surface shrouded in mist.

"Now what?" Jessie sighed and rested her hands on her hips. "We're not going to get across that. You just breathe real good on those rocks and it's all over."

"We'll have to go back, or work our way down the ridge to the water. We won't be able to see a thing from down there. I don't see why we—"

"Mark," Jessie said suddenly, "Mark, what's that over there?" She pointed a few degrees to their right, two hundred feet down the slope.

Hunter looked. "A couple of dead trees, maybe," he muttered, "only they're kind of far out in the water . . . My God, Jessie, you're right—those are *masts!* There's maybe two, three ships anchored out there under the fog!"

"They're Burke's ships," Jessie said tightly. "And that cutter that passed us last night. Maksutova's cutter. It has to be." Something else caught her attention, something she hadn't noticed before. She squinted against the swirling tendrils of fog.

A breeze off the water swept ragged mist aside. "Christ—oh, Christ, Mark!" A ragged cry stuck in her throat. She stared in disbelief, the blood cold as ice in her veins. It was Ki, and she was certain he was dead. He was hanging by his arms from the topmast of Maksutova's ship.

Chapter 19

The camp was some twenty yards from shore. There were two large tents set up in the trees to Jessie's left and bedrolls scattered nearby. Three evening cookfires were going in the draw and she could smell the tantalizing aroma of fresh coffee. As she watched, one of Burke's men spilled grease on the fire. A yellow tongue of flame leaped four feet into the air; the man cursed and stepped back and his friends laughed. A moment later, Jessie heard steak start to sizzle in a skillet.

As near as she and Hunter could tell, there were twenty or twenty-five men in the camp. They came and went at will, drifting down to the shore and wandering off in the trees, so there was no way to tell for sure. And no way at all to guess how many men might sleep on the ships at night. The fog was still thick, but Jessie and Hunter were sure there were four vessels in all. They could see the dim yellow halos of light through the mist. Maksutova's cutter and one nearly like it that was Burke's—plus two smaller vessels Burke had brought north from Sitka with men and supplies.

Jessie had spotted Burke himself. He had walked to one of the fires and talked to his men, taken a cup of coffee, and pointed off to the west. The men had nodded and Burke had said something that made them laugh. They went back to their meals and Burke strolled back to his tent.

Maksutova was nowhere in sight. Which meant he was likely aboard his cutter. Jessie wished she knew for sure. It would change nothing—but she still wanted to know where he was.

A twig snapped behind her and Jessie turned and saw Hunter move out of the fog behind her and to the left. She eased back down off her perch and joined him in a thick stand of trees. Fern grew waist-high on the forest floor. A million droplets of water beaded the dark fronds. The water felt icy cold against Jessie's cheek.

"They've got six horses back behind the tents," Hunter reported, "which means Burke brought 'em on one of his boats. There are five dories down by the water. Nobody's guarding them. They're just there, pulled halfway out of the water."

"Good," Jessie nodded. "That means they aren't worried about company. That makes it a lot easier—nobody'll think twice if one's missing." She turned and looked squarely at Hunter. "I'm going to say this again, Mark. I know you won't listen but I'm sayin' it anyway. You don't have to do this for me. I've got to get his body back. I don't intend to leave him up there on that mast. I'm going to do it and I'd just as soon you wouldn't tell me it's a damn fool thing to do. I already know that. There's no reason for you to have any part of this."

"All right." Hunter nodded without expression. "You finished?"

"Yes, I'm finished."

"Then we're wasting time sitting here." He pulled himself erect and helped her up. Jessie slid her hands around his shoulders and kissed him warmly. He held her a long moment, pressing his body against her, and then they turned and moved silently through the trees toward the shore.

Jessie sat in the bow of the boat, the rifle across her knees; Hunter rowed, his oars dipping soundlessly into the water. She

154

leaned into the dark, trying to penetrate the fog with all her senses. She could see the dim glow of the lanterns, hear the creak of timber and the water lapping up against the hull. The cutter appeared and then vanished, a long gray shadow close to the water, its skeletal mast lost in the fog.

When she'd seen him, glimpsed Ki for an instant from the ridge, all the fear and sorrow in the world had welled up inside her. It had lasted for a moment, the single beat of her heart. Then, strangely, she had felt nothing at all. Something deep within her told her feeling would destroy her, would keep her from what she had to do. Sorrow and tears could come later— if she were still alive to experience such emotion. Now, there was room for nothing but cold, purposeful anger. She would do this one thing. Nothing mattered but that. She would get Ki from Maksutova's ship and take him home. She would take him home and she would bury him next to her father on the Circle Star ranch. If she had to, she would walk from Alaska back to Texas. If anyone wanted to stop her they'd have to kill her. And when it was over, she would come back and find Kodiak Burke—Burke and the man who had murdered her friend.

"Jessie—*Jessie!*"

She jerked up, Hunter's harsh whisper sweeping her thoughts aside. The dark hull loomed dead ahead. She leaned out quickly and pressed her hands against the slick wet planking to keep the dory from bumping. Hunter lashed the boat under the overhanging stretch of the bow. If the current didn't shift, the line would stay taut and keep the boat from scraping against the hull. Still, if anyone decided to lean over the railing and look down . . .

Hunter went first, hand over hand up a line that hung from the bow. He knew there'd be a handy rope ladder somewhere midship, but they didn't dare take the chance. Jessie passed the Winchester up to Hunter, pulled herself up the line, and felt a strong grip bring her aboard.

For a long moment, they crouched in shadow forward. Wraithlike tendrils of fog crept over the ship. Jessie could see the mainmast, the white-painted bridge, and behind that, the dark column of the high stack. A lantern hung slowly at Jessie's shoulder, twenty feet to the left. Fog blurred the light but it was there. They'd simply have to avoid its dim aura. If they tried to put it out, someone would likely notice and come out to get it going again.

A man walked out on the main deck, lit his pipe, and flipped the match into the water. He looked out into the fog a long moment and went inside. Hunter touched Jessie's shoulder and nodded, then moved aft in a crouch.

The mainmast was halfway between the bow and the bridge. Jessie felt the hard, wet wood with the palm of her hand. She looked up, afraid of what she might see. The top of the mast was shrouded in fog. There were footholds in the mast. It would be easy enough to climb.

"No," Hunter said firmly in her ear. "You can get up there, but you can't bring him down. It's as simple as that."

"Mark—"

Hunter pulled away and disappeared, vanishing up the mast and into the fog. Jessie squatted on her heels, keeping the bulk of the mast between herself and the bridge. For a heart-stopping moment, she wondered if she'd taken time ashore to lever a shell into the chamber of the rifle. She couldn't remember at all and didn't dare do it now.

God, where are you Mark? It seemed as if he'd been gone forever. Something moved on the bridge. Jessie blinked, rubbed a sleeve across her eyes, and raised the Winchester to her waist. Whatever it was disappeared. Maybe it was nothing at all. It was easy to imagine things in the fog. She heard something and gripped the bulk of the mast. Glancing straight up, she saw the dark shadow moving ponderously toward her from above. The shadow was distorted, misshapen. Hunter, bringing Ki's body down on his shoulder. She tore her eyes away and searched the bridge, the decking in between. If anyone was about, they couldn't miss him coming down.

Suddenly he was beside her, easing Ki's limp form to the deck. It was the moment she'd dreaded most; she would have to see him and know that he was gone. She touched his cold cheeks, brushed strands of wet black hair from his face. His skin was so pale, all the color gone—A terrible cry welled up in her throat. She clamped a hand to her mouth and screamed inside. *His eyes—oh God, his eyes are still open, staring. Ki, Ki!*

"Jessie—damn it; Jessie, listen to me!" Hunter gripped her arms until they hurt, twisted her shoulders, and forced her to face him. "Jessie, he's not dead. He's alive. He's hurt bad but he's alive."

"What, what?" She stared, uncomprehending, unable to make sense of his words. "No, no I know he's dead. He's dead, Mark." She touched Ki's face again, imagined she saw a muscle twitch at the corner of his mouth. He brought his eyes into focus, tried to force his lips into a smile. Tears welled in Jessie's eyes and scalded her cheeks. Her hands shook and she lifted his head and pressed it against her breasts.

"Ki, oh Lord, Ki, what have they done to you!"

"I'm—be all right, Jessie . . ." His voice made Jessie's skin crawl. It was made of raw metal scraping stone. "I'm—on a ship . . . that's right, isn't it?"

"Yes, Ki. We'll get you off. We have a boat. Ki, what did they do with Natalia? Do you know?"

"Natalia . . ." The name sent a shadow across his face. It was clear he was trying to think. "Natalia . . . she's—somewhere . . . Maksutova . . ."

Jessie's eyes darted to Hunter and back to Ki. "Here, Ki? Do you think she's here? On this ship?"

". . . on this ship. Yes." His eyes were full of pain and desperation. "Natalia . . ."

Jessie touched his brow. "We'll find her, Ki. If she's here we'll find her." She turned to face Hunter. "We can't just leave him. If someone finds him here . . ."

"Stay with him. I'll have a look."

Jessie sighed and shook her head. "That'd take forever. Mark, we don't even know where to start." She looked down at Ki. His eyes met hers and she knew what he was thinking. He cared a great deal for the girl and wanted desperately to see her safe. Still, his first loyalty was to Jessie. He didn't want her to risk her life further. The pain of this was tearing him apart.

Jessie leaned down and kissed him. "I'll be back. I'll be

157

back, Ki." He said something she didn't understand. Jessie touched him once more and followed Hunter through the fog toward the bridge.

They worked their way aft, down the starboard side of the cutter. A door opened ahead and Hunter shoved Jessie flat against the deck. A man walked out of a cabin not three feet away. He looked aft a moment, then turned and started back inside. Jessie gripped Hunter's arm. The man suddenly stopped, whirled around, and looked right at them. His mouth opened to sound the alarm and Hunter came off the deck, brought his fist up from the floor, and struck the man under the jaw. The man sighed and crumpled. Hunter caught him and broke his fall, grabbed him under the shoulders, and dragged him inside.

Jessie searched the deck, listening for any sound, then followed Hunter in. A narrow passageway led halfway amidships then turned abruptly forward. A lantern glowed somewhere past the turn. A cabin door stood open to the right. Jessie peered inside and nodded to Hunter. Hunter dragged the limp form inside. Jessie stood at the door. A moment later, Hunter came up beside her. He had a short-barreled Smith & Wesson .38 in his hand and a broad-bladed knife stuck in his belt.

"He'll stay out for a while," he whispered. "I stuffed a bandanna in his mouth and tied him up with a sheet. It'll have to do."

They worked their way down the passage, Jessie walking ahead with the rifle while Hunter checked the cabins. Two were empty. A man's loud snore came from a third. The door of the first cabin past the turn stood slightly ajar. The acrid odor of sweat, the smell of dark tobacco hung on the air. Inside, there was an unmade bunk, a table bolted to the floor. A faded shirt hung over a chair. Jessie stared at the shirt. Something cold knotted up in her belly. Her fingers cut into Hunter's arm and he looked and saw it, too. The shirt was enormous, too big for an ordinary man. It took all the courage Jessie could muster to keep from turning away, bolting and running from the cabin.

"Easy, easy," said Hunter. He cast a wary look down the passageway, started out again, and then stopped. His eyes darted to the far corner of the cabin. Jessie saw it, too. There was another door, louvered with wooden slats. Hunter stepped in front of the hanging lamp, blocking the light and casting the door in shadow. The narrow spaces between the slats glowed with an eerie light of their own. Jessie shot Hunter a questioning look. *What the hell was it—what made a light like that?*

Jessie moved back to the passageway, peered outside, and nodded to Hunter. Hunter held the pistol at his waist, grasped the handle of the louvered door, and thrust it open quickly. He bent his legs at the knees, held the weapon out straight from his shoulders, and swept it about the room.

"Christ Jesus!" His eyes went wide and the pistol dropped slowly to his side. Jessie moved up beside him. A chill started at the base of her spine and rose to the back of her neck. The deck was crowded with candles, hundreds of white ship's candles. They were stuck in the necks of bottles, set in saucers and broken plates, and melted to the planking itself. The tiny cabin was stifling with their heat. The candles were lined neatly in rows, leading to the far wall of the room. Natalia Shelikhov hung from the wooden bulkhead. Spikes had been driven into the wall, and Natalia's wrists were tied to the spikes straight out from her shoulders. Her bare feet touched the floor. Her head was covered in some faded white material, old lace or yellowed gauze. The cloth was tangled about her throat and fell in tattered strands about her breasts. Her head sagged limply between her shoulders; she was naked except for the ragged pieces of cloth. Her slender form glistened with beads of moisture. The candles turned her flesh to copper and gold.

Understanding struck Jessie like a blow. The candles, the bizarre imitation of a veil; there was even a Russian icon on the wall, crudely snipped from a piece of tin. The tiny room was a nightmare chapel, and Natalia was the bride. The only thing missing was the groom.

Natalia raised her head and groaned. Jessie came to her senses and moved to her side. Hunter was already there, slicing the bonds from the girl's wrists.

"It's all right," Jessie whispered, "you're all right." She turned and stepped quickly back in Maksutova's cabin, her

159

fingers on the trigger of the rifle. She searched the room for Natalia's clothes, found nothing and ripped a blanket from the bunk, backed away and tossed the blanket to Hunter. Hunter helped the girl out of the cabin and into the passage.

"Can you make it?" Jessie asked. "Can you walk?"

Natalia's eyes were wide with alarm. "I—yes, I'm all right. Ki, is he—?"

"We've got him," Hunter told her. "We're all going to get the hell out of here. Just take it easy and stay close."

"Maksutova," Jessie asked, "where is he? Do you know?"

"I don't know," Natalia trembled, "God, he's here somewhere. Don't let him find me—please!"

Jessie bit her lip and led the way down the corridor. The path was clear back to the outer door, past the cabin where Hunter had left the unconscious gunman. Jessie searched the darkness. Fog crept into the passage. She looked back at Hunter, stepped outside, and went low, sweeping the rifle in every direction. Natalia shivered and Hunter gripped her shoulders.

We'll make it, Jessie told herself. *It's all right now; we'll make it.*

The fog seemed thicker than ever. Jessie prayed that it would hold. They moved away from the bridge, back to the mainmast. Ki had pulled himself shakily to his knees. Natalia made a sound in her throat and started for him. Hunter motioned her to silence.

"Help him up," he said. "Put your shoulder under his arm and keep him going."

"Yes, yes," Natalia muttered. Hunter helped her get Ki to his feet. Ki's face contorted in pain.

"Get them to the bow," Hunter whispered to Jessie. "I'll cover from here until you're over. And stay clear of that lantern."

Jessie shook her head. "That's no good, Mark. You're going to have to get Ki over the side. Natalia and I can't do it. Go on—I'll do the covering job."

Hunter paused; he realized she was right but he didn't like it. "Just watch it, all right? And damn it, Jessie, don't hang around any longer than you have to!"

Jessie pushed him on his way. He turned and vanished toward the bow. Jessie went to her knees and searched the fog. She could feel her heart pounding. Every shadow was a specter, every creak of the ship's timbers a footstep moving toward her across the deck.

"Get off this thing," she said between her teeth. "Get them *out* of here, Mark."

The hoarse cry startled her and nearly brought her to her feet. A door slammed open. Another voice answered the first. Jessie cursed under her breath. It had to be the man Mark had tossed into the cabin. *Damn you—why couldn't you stay under another minute!*

A burst of fire came from just below the bridge. Jessie saw the quick flashes of brightness through the fog. The shots went wild, off to her right. They were guessing. They didn't know where she was. Not yet. A figure suddenly appeared, darting across the top of the bridge. The man stopped, turned in her direction, and pointed. A pistol cracked twice from the main deck. Jessie held her fire and darted to better cover. Lead splintered wood at her heels. Jessie leaped to one side, rolled, came quickly to her knees.

All right, she thought grimly, *that's about close enough*. She saw the shadow moving toward her out of the fog, let out a breath, and squeezed the Winchester's trigger. The shadow cried out and went sprawling. Jessie moved—a hail of bullets chewed wood where she had been. She backed quickly toward the bow. Two men came at her from the port side of the ship. Jessie tossed three rapid shots in their direction. The men scattered for cover. She bent to a crouch and backed away. A terrible sound reached her ears, coming from nowhere and everywhere at once. She whirled about, the blood going cold in her veins. The sound brought a nightmare picture to her mind—the lean flanks of a wolf, the smell of wet fur. She saw him then, coming at her across the deck, his giant form sweeping the fog aside. She backed off, fighting the awful fear that threatened to turn her legs to lead. She brought the rifle to her shoulder and squeezed. The firing pin snapped on an empty chamber. Jessie nearly cried out. Maksutova heard the sound

161

of metal on metal and laughed. Jessie backed off. Her shoulder hit something solid. Light swung crazily over her head. Without thinking she reached up and jerked the heavy ship's lantern free, stumbled back, and hurled the thing straight at Maksutova. Glass shattered. The sharp odor of kerosene filled the air. A searing ball of fire lit the deck. Maksutova stopped in his tracks as the yellow sheet of flame leaped up in his face. He howled and turned in a circle, flailing his arms against his chest. Jessie shrank back in horror. Maksutova stumbled, fell, picked himself up, and lumbered awkwardly to the far side of the deck, shrieking in pain and terror. His legs hit the port side railing; wood splintered and he stepped over the edge in a flaming pyre.

Jessie came to her senses, turned, and ran for the bow. Once more, gunfire shattered the silence behind her. Without looking back, she leaped the low railing and dived into the dark water below.

★
Chapter 20

The cold water sent a sudden shock through her body. She struggled for the surface. The weight of her boots and the heavy fleece jacket pulled her deeper. She was dimly aware that she still clutched the rifle in her hand. It dragged her steadily downward but she stubbornly clung to the barrel, refused to let it go. Her lungs threatened to burst. She clawed frantically for the surface. In an awful moment of panic, she was sure she was going the wrong way—down instead of up.

Lights began to explode before her eyes. Something closed painfully about her wrists and her head suddenly broke through the water. She cried out and sucked in air, choked on water and retched, the taste of salt and bile filling her mouth. Hunter shouted something she couldn't hear, tugged at her shoulders and threw her roughly against the side of the dory. Jessie held on, gagged, and spat water. Hunter pulled himself back in the boat, went to his knees, and helped her aboard. Jessie saw Hunter toss his knife to Natalia; the girl scrambled forward, and seconds later the dory was free. Hunter bent to the oars and rowed frantically, each stroke bringing a quick explosion of air from his chest. Gunfire blossomed from the cutter. Natalia cried out and threw herself over Ki.

"Here, take this," Hunter shouted. He thrust the Smith & Wesson at Jessie. "You all right?"

Jessie didn't answer. Lead whined over her head. Bullets sprayed water to her right. Jessie held the pistol in both hands and fired twice at the bow of the cutter. The gunmen backed off, but only for an instant. A rifle opened up, coming dangerously close to the dory. Fog closed in and the cutter disappeared. Hunter veered sharply to the right. The men in the cutter fired steadily into the dark, blindly searching for a target.

"My God, what's that?" Hunter sat up straight, let the oars sag in the water, and stared in the direction of the cutter. Pale orange light flickered through the thick wall of mist, growing brighter as he watched.

"Maksutova," Jessie said shakily, "I threw a lantern at him. He went over the side."

Hunter let a breath explode through his teeth. "That isn't all you did. Jessie, the whole damn ship's goin' up!" He glanced over his shoulder and started rowing again. "The shore's that way, I think. If I keep going right it'll take us away from the camp."

Jessie nodded. She could see lanterns glowing all around her in the distance. The men on the other vessels had seen the flames. Fog or no fog, it wouldn't be long until there were plenty of other dories in the water—from the ships and from Burke's camp ashore.

"Is—is it true what you said?" Natalia stretched back to grip Jessie's arm. "Maksutova—he is gone?"

"The lantern set him afire," Jessie told her. "I saw him go over the side."

"Thank God!" Natalia closed her eyes and clutched the blanket about her shoulders. "He was insane, a monster. I cannot tell you the things he—"

"Don't," Jessie said gently. She rested her hand on the girl's shoulder. "Don't, Natalia." She moved past her, closer to Ki. He sat up and took her hands between his own.

164

"You look like you got chewed up and spit out," Jessie told him. She forced a smile and let it fade. "How are you? What did he do to you, Ki?"

"He didn't break anything," Ki told her. He glanced down at his knees, looked up, and met her eyes. "He did things that hurt, things that kept the pain going. He was good at that. He could have gone a lot further but he didn't. He kept me alive. I don't know why but he did."

"I know," Natalia said suddenly. Her voice trembled as she spoke. "He–he kept me there, with those terrible candles . . . he never even touched me, Jessie. He just looked at my body all the time and told me—told me what we would do with each other when we were married."

"Married!" Ki's eyes went wide.

"I told you, he is crazy. He was going to take me back to Sitka. He would make the priest at St. Michael's marry us." She bit her lip and looked at Ki. "This is why he was keeping you alive. He told me. You would watch our wedding. Then he would—" Natalia shook her head quickly. "He told me the things he would do to you then."

Ki's face twisted in anger. "They shoot mad dogs and Burke lets that son of a bitch run loose!"

"Hold it down back there," Hunter warned them. "We've got company."

Jessie heard it, then—the sound of oars, a boat slicing through the water. A moment later she saw the lights, lanterns winking out of the fog. The lanterns were high above the water; she guessed the men were holding them on poles. The fog lifted for an instant and Jessie held her breath. Her nails dug into Ki's arms. She saw the dory loaded with men from the camp. The lanterns striped their rifles with yellow light. Another boat was off to the right. Jessie looked at Hunter and he gave her a sheepish grin. He lowered his oars back in the water and rowed silently for the shore. Over her shoulder, Jessie could still see the glow of the burning ship.

"It's the only thing we can do," said Jessie. She squinted at Hunter's crudely drawn map in the dirt. "We head northeast

165

up Yakutat Bay, keeping to the cover of the trees, staying close enough to the water so we can see what's going on there." She glanced up at Hunter and Natalia. "If you're right, maybe we'll run into one of those Russian trading camps and get some help."

"I am sure there are *odinotshkas,* factories, near the mouth of one of the rivers that flows into the bay. The workers fish and trade with the Indians. My uncle spoke of these places."

"Good," Jessie nodded. "If we can find one of those, we can decide whether to go on east or turn south. Ki, what do you think?"

"I wish I knew the country," he said grimly.

"Forget the country," said Hunter. "It's rough going any direction we pick. You want my opinion, I think I'd rather stick close to the coast and go south, instead of tryin' the St. Elias Mountains."

"We've got to get out of here before we can think about going anywhere else," Jessie reminded them. She glanced back over her shoulder. They had waited near the shore through the night, pulling the dory as far onto the rocks as they could and covering it with branches. They could hear Burke's men searching the bay, see the lights of their boats in the distance.

The fog lifted at four in the morning and they made their way up through the trees; Ki tried to keep going, but he had little strength for the climb. By daylight, they had moved maybe three or four miles down the bay. Jessie guessed they were five hundred yards above the water. The sight to the north was awesome, a fantasy straight out of some dream. Less than a mile away, the high, sheer wall of the Malaspina glacier loomed over the forest. The first rays of the sun turned the ice pale rose, the color fading quickly to glaring white. Past the cold face of the glacier, stretching to the north, was the surface of the ice floe itself. Beyond, lost in blood-red clouds, was the peak of St. Elias. Hunter said no one was certain how high the mountain might be—eighteen thousand feet, maybe even more.

"There's no use hanging around here," Hunter said. He stood and stretched, walked a few yards, and peered south through the trees toward the bay. "I don't see any ships—but that doesn't mean they aren't there. Burke's men haven't gone to sleep. I'd guess they've found the dory by now and know which way we're headed."

"You said they had six horses," Ki spoke up. "They will send the horses ahead to find where we are, then signal the others to come."

"That's it, all right," Hunter agreed. He offered Ki a hand; Ki nodded and waved him off, bringing himself painfully to his feet. Jessie bit her lip and looked away. She could read her friend well and could know how much hurt he was holding back. His will alone was keeping him going. If they had to run, move very quickly, his will simply wouldn't be enough.

Natalia huddled close by his shoulder. Jessie knew the girl had scarcely left his side since they'd escaped in the dory. She had no clothing except for her blanket. Jessie had torn strips from one side and helped her wind them around her feet. Then they'd tied the makeshift shoes with leather cord. It wasn't much, but it kept her from tearing her flesh on the rocky ground.

When it happened, Hunter ran up from the rear and calmly gave them the news. No one was surprised. They'd been expecting it all along.

"I saw them. They're coming up with the horses directly behind us. Probably men on foot farther back." He looked past Jessie's shoulder. "There's more. One of the ships is offshore right below. They're putting men ashore in small boats. We can't go back. If we move on the way we're going now, we're going to run right into that second bunch."

"Doesn't leave us much choice," Ki said evenly.

"No, it doesn't." Hunter nodded to the north. "That way."

Natalia's eyes grew wide. "That's the glacier. We can't go up that!"

"We can't go anywhere else," Ki told her.

Hunter studied the sheer wall of ice. "When we were up a little higher back there, it looked as if the trees made kind of a *Y* to the north. Maybe we can get onto the floe from fairly easy ground."

And if we can't, Jessie thought, *we're backed up there in*

167

a dead end. That's where Kodiak Burke will find us. There was no need to say it aloud. The others all knew it. She could read it in their eyes.

A quarter hour later, the trees began to thin. The steep forested slope gave way to a scared, rocky surface, land where the glacier had retreated and left the terrain raw and broken, veined with a network of ragged fissures. They could see the ice ahead, to the left and to the right, closer than a mile in every direction. The way ahead was ribboned with treacherous glacial debris piled in long, twisted lines that stretched the length of the slope. Sometimes the drifts were fine as sand with stones no bigger than marbles. To the east, the debris was a collection of boulders bigger than houses.

When Jessie turned, she saw the horses, working their way up past the trees into the open. Her throat went dry at the sight.

"God, they're so close," she said aloud. "They're right up on us!"

"Close enough," Hunter snapped. "Come on, we can't stay here." He looked at Jessie. "I've got three rounds in this pistol I took off that fella on the cutter. What about you?"

"Nine," Jessie said dully. "That's it. I had more than that, but I lost some rounds when I took a swim. Mark, we aren't going to scare anybody to death."

Hunter turned away and started up the slope. Jessie fell back to help Ki. She nodded at Natalia, and the girl reluctantly left his side. She was clearly exhausted, but didn't want to quit.

"Are you all right?" Jessie asked. "Foolish question, huh?"

Ki showed her a painful smile. "Yes. Foolish question." He met her eyes and turned away. "I can't go much more. I know my body. I know what I can do."

"Ki—"

"No." His dark eyes blazed with determination. "We don't need to speak of this, Jessie. We know each other too well. You are thinking you will not leave me behind, and I am telling you that you will. You will not waste your life on such a gesture. If you do, you waste my life as well. You leave me with nothing but shame."

168

"Shut up," said Jessie, "I don't want to hear any of this."

Ki started to speak. Shots rang out from below, the sound rolling up the slope and echoing like thunder across the ice field again and again. Jessie looked back and saw the horsemen inching up the incline to her right. The man in the lead was still a good four hundred yards down the hill, but Jessie was certain she recognized Burke's stocky figure in the saddle. Behind him, she could see the men on foot, swarming up the rocky draw after the riders.

Hunter called out and waved her forward. Natalia ran back to help Jessie with Ki.

"I will not have this," Ki said through his teeth. "I will not, Jessie!"

"Yeah, I heard you before," Jessie told him.

The rocky hill narrowed past a field of enormous glacial boulders. A few yards beyond was the ice, stretching up forever toward Mount St. Elias. The edge of the ice curled down in a steep, thirty degree angle toward the draw.

Hunter ran back and gave Jessie an irritated look. "That's it; there's nowhere else to go."

"They can't take the horses up that," Jessie said.

"They'd be crazy as hell to try." He looked past Jessie to Ki. "I know what you're thinking and it isn't going to happen. No one's staying behind. We're all going to climb that thing. You're going up with me. I don't think you're feeling good enough right now to stop me."

Ki shook his head. "Hunter, I don't want this."

"And if it was me, you'd leave me behind, right?"

"That's got nothing to—damn it, Hunter!" Ki's mouth stretched in pain as Hunter bent suddenly and laid his shoulder in Ki's belly, then stood quickly with Ki over his back. Ki moaned. Jessie reached up and brushed hair out of his face. Hunter stalked woodenly to the edge of the ice field slope and started climbing.

The lip of the glacial slope leveled some twenty yards above the rocky draw. Hunter sighed and eased Ki to the ground, then went to his knees and sucked in air.

"It's not so bad up ahead," he told Ki. "Can you do it?"

169

"I'll do it," Ki said grimly. "Just get me on my feet."

Jessie ran back a few yards and looked down the slope. A rider glanced up and saw her and loosed a volley. Jessie ducked and went back to the others.

"They're coming. Burke and the others who had horses. They'll be right where we're standing in a few minutes. The rest are working up the draw. Mark, there must be twenty or thirty of them."

Hunter nodded. "We'll cross over laterally to the west." He pointed into the glare. There was a dark spur of rock thrusting twenty feet up through the floe. It stretched up the glacial slope in a nearly straight line, a mark as black as coal against the ice. "Let's get over there fast," Hunter said. "It'll give us good cover. They'll be in the open and we can hold 'em off, give them something to think about."

Jessie looked at Hunter. He wouldn't meet her eyes. *Hold them off with what? It ends right here. This is where it stops.*

"You're going straight across instead of climbing because of me," Ki said sharply. "You might get to the mountains if you cut east."

"You know better than that," said Jessie. "Without cover we can't make it to the east." Ki muttered under his breath. Natalia and Jessie eased under his shoulders and followed Hunter.

The ice field was treacherous, solid one moment and then slashed with deep crevasses the next. There was no way to hurry, no way to reach the rocky spur any faster. Jessie risked a look over her shoulder. At any instant, she expected to see Burke and his crew appear at the top of the slope. A quick burst of fire, easy targets nearly standing still on the ice . . .

She let her gaze follow the dark spine of rock up the slopes of St. Elias. The line curved slightly and then vanished. Another ridge crossed it, just below the point where it disappeared. The second ridge was broken; the ice appeared for an instant, then the ridge surfaced again. Jessie looked away. Almost at once, something drew her eyes back to the sight. It looked familiar for some reason she couldn't fathom. She shook her head and frowned. Maybe she'd seen a mountainside like it somewhere before. In Montana, the Colorado Rockies—

It struck her, then, like a physical blow. She stopped in her tracks and stared. The Aleut! The old Indian who had scrawled his crazy symbol on the walls of Hiram Platte's loft. There it was, the drawing come to life in the dark configuration on the mountain. It was identical, even to the ragged, broken line that crossed the vertical slash!

"Jessie!" Hunter turned and waved his arm frantically in her direction. "Damn it, Jessie, what are you waiting for!"

Jessie came to her senses and pulled her gaze away from the mountain. The shot rang out behind her. Another followed the first until it sounded as if Burke had hauled a Gatling gun up the glacier. Lead tugged at the collar of her jacket. Natalia cried out, and Jessie pushed Ki and the girl to the ground. She leaped aside and rolled, came to her feet, and put herself between Ki and Natalia until the girl got Ki to his feet. She paused for an instant, tried to get off a shot. The withering volley of fire drove her back. Hunter started back to help. Jessie waved him on. Natalia and Ki reached the dark spur of rock. Ki tried to climb and slipped. Lead made geysers of ice at his feet. Natalia climbed past him and gripped his hands, frantically tugging him over the edge.

Jessie ran. A ragged crevasse loomed directly in her path. She started to veer around it, knew there wasn't time. She leaped and went sprawling on her belly. The rifle slipped out of her grip. Her legs began to slide toward the gaping hole; she cried out and clawed desperately at the ice. Hunter was suddenly there. He gripped her wrists and jerked her back to safety. Jessie struggled to her feet, scooped up the rifle, and ran. Gunfire stitched the ice at her heels as she scrambled up the rocky face of the spur, then sprawled on the other side and gasped for air.

Hunter poked his head over the top and snapped off a shot with his pistol before heavy fire drove him back. Jessie looked at Ki. His face was splotched with color. A thin line of white etched his lips.

"I'm going up a few yards," Hunter said tightly. "I've got two shots left. I'll draw 'em off you for a minute. Get in a couple of rounds. We'll take as many of the bastards as we can." He held her eyes a moment. "You want the rifle or you want me to do it?"

"I'll do it." She tried to smile. "I'm as good a shot as you are—as long it's not a buffalo gun."

"I wish to hell I had it right now," Hunter said grimly. He nodded and moved off. Jessie waited. Hunter leaned over the top and fired twice. Burke's men answered with a volley that dusted stone at Hunter's head. Jessie raised up on her knees, picked a target, and fired. A man went down. She squeezed off another shot and missed. Every gun turned in her direction.

The sight she'd seen over the spur was still a stark, frightening image in her mind. Burke's men were coming at them over the ice, spread in a ragged line like troopers advancing on an enemy position. She might stop two, maybe three—no more than that. Hunter's revolver was empty.

Lead whined overhead. A man barked out a command. Jessie was certain it was Burke. She looked at Hunter and Natalia. Her eyes met Ki's and held them. She levered another shell into the Winchester. Seven left, if she'd counted right. What difference did it make? Taking a deep breath, she gripped the trigger guard and raised her head again. The weapon nearly jerked out of her hands. Her knees buckled and she reached out frantically to keep from falling. For a second she thought she'd been hit. She ran a hand shakily over her breasts and stared at Hunter.

The strange, sickening motion struck again, this time harder than the first. Jessie's eyes went wide. Now she was dead certain—the earth had *moved* under her feet! She opened her mouth to speak. A terrible, wrenching sound split the air. It began like the blast of a cannon, rose in pitch, and echoed sharply down the mountain, rippling the ground as it thundered by.

"It's the guns," Ki said sharply, "all the damn guns going off!"

Hunter nodded. He raised his head carefully over the edge and Jessie joined him. Burke's men stood frozen, their eyes locked on something to the north. Jessie followed their glance. The main floe of the glacier snaked down the mountain some two thousand feet up the slope. The glacial drift was higher as it twisted off to the west. As Jessie watched, a few loose stones and shards of ice rattled down the side of the mountain. A harsh, tearing sound started within the earth, then stopped just as quickly as it had begun.

Kodiak Burke turned angrily, shouted at his men, and waved them forward. His voice echoed over the ice. The men looked at each other, glanced furtively up the mountain. A few took hesitant steps over the ice. The others stood still. Even from a distance, Jessie could see the rage twist Burke's features. He turned, then, as if he guessed her thoughts, raised a heavy pistol, and emptied it in her direction.

Jessie held her breath as the sound of the weapon died away. Burke threw back his head, laughed at the mountain, and started for the spur of rock again. His men hesitated an instant, then moved in a ragged line with him.

"Okay, mister," Jessie muttered tightly, "that's damn near close enough." She brought the stock of the Winchester to her cheek, let out a breath, and let the sights come to rest on Burke's chest. She held the position a long moment, then raised the barrel higher, paused, and raised it higher still, until the high slope of the mountain was her target.

Hunter's eyes went wide with alarm. "Jessie, for God's sake !"

Jessie didn't answer. She squeezed her shots off slowly, taking all the time in the world to lever fresh shells into the chamber. When the rifle clicked empty, she lowered it to her waist, opened her hands, and let it clatter over the rocks.

Kodiak Burke stopped in his tracks. He looked right at Jessie, his dark eyes burning into hers over the distance. Jessie held her breath. There was no sound on the mountain. Even the wind seemed to have died. Then, Jessie felt the first tremble, a slight motion rising up from the rocks under her feet. The motion and the sound began to grow, as if some great sleeping beast were waking up beneath the earth.

One of Burke's men dropped his weapon, turned, and bolted. Then another and another, until the whole line of gunmen turned and fled. Only Kodiak Burke stood his ground. Jessie looked

173

past him and saw it coming. The wall of ice seemed to blur, then break itself free with a noise like splintering wood. From two thousand feet down the mountain, the rumbling white mass seemed agonizingly slow. Burke knew what was behind him; he never moved, he never turned to look.

Chapter 21

When it was over, when the earth stopped trembling and the thunder turned to silence, they brought themselves shakily to their feet and stared in disbelief at the sight. Everything east of the ridge was gone. Only the rocky spur on which they stood was unchanged; its roots were a part of the bedrock of the mountain. Tons of glacial ice and stone had carved a raw, gaping wound five hundred yards wide down the slope. Everything in its path had vanished. The avalanche had swept past the ice floe itself and funneled down the narrow, rocky ravine they had followed to the glacier. The earth was scoured clean and the trees were gone clear to the bay. Ice and stone and dirt formed a slide that extended fifty yards into the water. There was no sign of the cutter that had brought Burke's men down the bay.

"There are still those two smaller ships—the ones he used to haul men and supplies up from Sitka," said Jessie. "They'll come and see what happened."

Hunter nodded, his eyes still locked on the scene below.

"Whoever's left isn't going to come looking up here. Not after they see that."

Jessie was silent a long moment. She looked past Ki and Natalia, at the peak of St. Elias. "There's something else," she said evenly, "something we have to do." She told them, then, what she'd seen as they crossed the ice, that she was certain the spur of rock where they stood was a part of the Aleut's crude drawing.

Natalia stared at Jessie and shook her head in alarm. "The Indian said nothing of such a thing to my uncle. Nothing!"

"I know he didn't," said Jessie. "We'll likely never know why he kept it to himself. Maybe he figured on asking for more money, and Maksutova scared him off before he could get back to Nikolai. Maybe he just wanted to hold on to part of the secret. I don't know."

"You think this cross has something to do with the wreck of the *Okhotsk?*" Ki asked.

"I think it could, Ki. That's all I can tell you."

Hunter squinted up the mountain. "Makes sense. He could've used this spur as a marking point, if the wreck's really somewhere close. Won't take a long time to find out. This rock goes up maybe another quarter mile, and there's only the west bar of the cross left. If the wreck was on that side, it's gone now."

Hunter was gone for more than an hour. When he returned he said there was nothing at all to see. Jessie was disappointed but said nothing. They started down the side of the mountain, following the line of the rocky spur. The spur disappeared two hundred yards down the slope, just before the trees began again. Hunter said he wondered how in hell they were going to get across the slide and work east into the bay toward the Russian trading posts.

They saw it, lying directly in their path. The base of the spur pointed to the site like an arrow.

"My God," Jessie said in wonder. "It's there. It really happened, just like the old Indian said it did."

No one answered. They stood for a long time, gazing at a legend come to life.

The *Okhotsk* was half-buried in an icy crevasse. The dark

hull was twisted and broken, the stern leaning a good five degrees left of the bow. The masts were sheared off just above the deck. Jessie looked past the wreck and down through the trees. Yakutat Bay was still nearly two hundred yards away. She shuddered, trying to imagine what it must have been like at that terrible moment some forty years before when the great Pacific typhoon lifted the ship up and out of the water and tossed it onto the glacier. It was a miracle there was anything left at all, one of the odd twists of nature that the storm had left the *Okhotsk* nearly intact instead of smashing it to splinters on the ice.

"I'm frightened," Natalia told Ki. "I don't know if I can go down there."

Ki squeezed her hand. "There is nothing here that can hurt you."

"I know that—but knowing it doesn't make the fear go away. It doesn't change what I am feeling."

It didn't take long to search the wreckage. In less than a half hour, they'd seen all there was to see. Hunter made torches of scraps of wood to light their way through the eerie passageways, the bridge, the crew's quarters, and the hold. Bits of chairs, tables, smashed crockery, and collapsed timbers were scattered everywhere. Jessie picked up a framed, yellowed picture of Tsar Nikolas I. He looked resplendent in his uniform and medals.

There were a few gnawed bones to remind them that men had died aboard the *Okhotsk*. Wolves had found the wreckage a generation before, but had left the place deserted since then.

There was no treasure in the hold, no hidden chests of gold.

Jessie, Hunter, Ki, and Natalia stood in the ruined cabin that had clearly belonged to Natalia's grandfather. The light from Hunter's torches smoked the rich timbered walls.

"Maybe the gold was torn free of the ship," Natalia said, "when the storm lifted the *Okhotsk* out of the water."

Jessie shook her head. "The cargo hold is intact, Natalia. Anyway, the ship didn't break up until it struck the glacier. If the gold was onboard, it'd still be here."

Natalia's face twisted in scorn. "You see, it is as I said in the beginning. It was a legend, a story. My uncle died for nothing. The whole thing was for nothing."

Ki went to her, but Natalia turned away. She wandered about her grandfather's cabin, touching the corner of a table, running her fingers over a fragment of glass. Once, she bent to the deck and picked up an ornate silver spoon. Ki stood back and watched her. He knew what she was doing. She was trying to see the cabin as it was, be where her grandfather had been.

Jessie and Hunter worked their way back up the narrow passageway to the bridge.

"The girl's right," Hunter said soberly. "The whole damn thing is a waste. It ends right here in a ship falling to pieces in a glacier. Like nothing had ever happened."

"No, that's not true, Mark." Jessie's eyes met his. Burke's dead. His death won't pay for Hiram Platte and Nikolai—or the Indian who's name I don't even know and all the other people the man murdered. But he's gone. And that gives us a chance to slow down the cartel in Alaska."

Hunter looked at her. "Slow them down. But that's all."

"I know what you're trying to say. It's like trying to hold back the typhoon that hit this place forty years ago. I know that. But I can't just quit trying."

Hunter didn't answer. Jessie studied the planes of his face, the deep lines at the corners of his eyes. Her hand touched the smooth wooden surface of the wall. There was a metal sextant still lodged on a shelf. A harpoon was clipped to a rack overhead. The polished shaft was five feet long, the sharpened steel head nearly two feet longer than that.

"Mark, you know why I'm here," Jessie said evenly. "I still don't know about you. Do you know that? You've never told me what you wanted, what you were after."

Hunter turned to face her. For an instant, a shadow crossed his features. "I'm sorry. I should have told you before now." He shrugged and looked at his hands. "It's no big mystery, Jessie. There isn't any Prussian cartel or anything like that. Just me—and a brother who was the only family I had."

Hunter stared at the flickering torch. "He was a gunsmith.

He lived outside New York City. He was good at what he did and he finally opened up his own arms factory. Made some of the finest pistols you ever saw. When his business got going real good, a man dropped by to see him and told him it'd be a good idea to take out a little insurance—just to make sure nothing happened. Bud, my brother, knew exactly what he was talking about. He kicked the man out on his ass. The man came back and brought his friends. They said they'd give Bud another chance to change his mind. Bud laughed in their faces. They hurt him. They didn't kill him; they just left him a cripple." Hunter's lips went taut. "Bud had a wife and a little boy. He was a man who loved living. He couldn't handle the way they'd left him. He shot himself a month later—with a pistol he'd made himself."

Jessie looked away. "Kodiak Burke comes from New York."

"Yes, he does. And he was living in the city when my brother was crippled. That was eight, nearly nine years ago now. Burke and a couple of others were running an extortion racket. He was small time then. Before he met up with your Prussian friends."

"And that's why you got close to Burke," said Jessie, "because you knew what he'd done to your brother."

"That's just it. I know and I don't know, Jessie!"

Jessie was taken aback by the sudden change in his appearance, the tortured look in his eyes. It was a part of Marcus Hunter she'd never seen before.

"Hell, I'm dead certain Burke is guilty as sin. I *know* he did it. I could have called him on it, had it over and done between us a long time ago. Only, I can't prove it was him, Jessie. I can't do that."

Hunter turned away and gripped the tarnished brass of the ship's wheel. "That's the other part of this thing," he went on. "I was sure I had Bud's killer a year after he died. I followed the man clear to Ohio and called him out. He laughed in my face. I shot him down. He didn't even have a gun. He was a dead ringer for Burke. Only he wasn't the right man, Jessie. He was a printer. He had a family. Like Bud." He looked wearily at Jessie. "I'm wanted for that killing. I guess they're still looking for me; I don't know."

"Oh Lord, Mark."

Hunter gave her a hollow laugh. "It isn't Mark, of course. Or Hunter either, for that matter."

"So you couldn't kill Burke—even though you knew."

"No," he said darkly, "I couldn't. I tried, but I couldn't make myself do it. All I could see was the face of the man I'd murdered. That's why I was hanging around Burke. I told myself I had to be sure this time. Maybe I never could have brought myself to do it. Hell, I don't know anymore." His hands clenched at his sides. "I'd stand there laughing with the bastard and drinking his imported brandy and knowing damn well what he'd done to Bud."

Jessie laid a hand on his arm. "That doesn't sound to me like a man who's branded himself a killer."

Hunter stared. "Are you sayin' I'm not? Didn't you hear what I said? I did it, Jessie."

"I heard. And you were wrong. You did a terrible thing. And it sounds to me as if you're paying for what you did a thousand times over. What do you want to do, Mark—go back to Ohio and hang? That won't bring back the man you shot."

Hunter's face twisted into a mocking smile. "That'd be the right thing to do now, wouldn't it? I wish I was that good a man. I'm not, Jessie. What do you think of that? I was wrong, but I don't want to pay for what I did. I want to stay alive."

"That's not too hard to understand," Jessie said gently. "And as I said, I think you're paying. I think you're paying plenty."

His eyes met hers. "That's not what the law says—that if you're sorry you don't have to hang."

"I'm not the law, Mark. I can't give you that answer. You'll have to do that yourself."

"I've been sending the man's family money since it happened, a lot of money."

"I'm not surprised. I think I know what kind of man you are."

"Do you? Then tell me. I'm not real sure, Jessie."

"I don't think the man who made love to me like you did is a man who isn't strong inside, a man who doesn't feel deep sadness—and deep joy, too."

180

"Jessie—"

Hunter started toward her then stopped. Natalia ducked under the narrow doorway onto the bridge. Ki was right behind her. Natalia's eyes were bright; she clutched a black metal box against her breast.

"It's the ship's log," she said intently, "I found it in my grandfather's cabin. His name is inside the cover!"

Jessie stood up straight. "Does it tell what happened—the storm, anything like that?"

"The storm is there," Natalia said soberly. "The beginning of it, at least. We guessed the truth about that. They tried to take cover in Yakutat Bay. There's no entry after that." She sat down on the floor and pulled the blanket about her shoulders, then opened the metal box, and took out the leather-bound log.

"This is the part that's important," she told the others. "The part I want you to hear." She opened the brittle pages, found the passage, and read aloud:

> *". . . . I anticipate no problems getting backing from other members of the Shelikhov family. When I return to Russia from Bolshaia Zeml'a—"*

Natalia looked up. "Great Land. That's what the old settlers called Alaska."

> *"—they will all be more than eager to join my venture when they see the rich samples I bring to show. There is enough gold to make it the richest strike the world has ever seen. I would stake my life on this."*

Hunter let out a breath. "There wasn't any gold on the ship. Your grandfather was talking about a strike. He found gold somewhere and he was going back home to get money to develop the field!"

"He told my grandmother there was gold, that we would all

be rich," Natalia said. "The gold was still in the ground, but my grandmother did not understand this." She looked up and smiled wearily at Ki. "Maybe she believed what she wanted to believe, yes? At any rate, it is how the story got started."

"Does he say anything about where the strike is?" Jessie asked.

"There is a map," said Natalia. "Here. He drew it near the front of his log."

Jessie, Hunter, and Ki crowded together and looked over the girl's shoulder. The map was meticulously drawn with draftsmanlike strokes of a fine pen. The page was covered with an intricate network of rivers and streams—the Stewart, the Yukon, a creek called the Klondike and hundreds more.

"I know where this is," said Hunter. "North of here. Couple of hundred miles. South of the divide."

Ki let the shadow of a grin cross his features. "Your grandfather was not a foolish man. He's drawn a map, but he doesn't show where the strike is to be found."

"Shouldn't be hard to pin it down," Hunter said dryly. "Only about forty thousand square miles, four or five hundred creeks and rivers. You want to go gold hunting, Ki?"

"I don't think so," Ki told him. "If there is gold there, someone else will have to find it."

Natalia grinned. "We don't have to wonder if it's there, Ki. There is gold, as my grandfather said. Look—" She reached into the metal box, scooped up something in her fist and held it high. When she opened her hand, two nuggets the size of walnuts lay in her palm.

"Holy Christ!" Hunter let a breath pass slowly between his teeth.

"When we get back to Sitka," Natalia said, "I am going to buy everyone the biggest steak dinner to be had. And wine. Yes, there should be wine, too."

"You can buy all the cattle in Alaska with that," said Ki, "and a herd of moose besides."

"Good." Natalia laughed and planted a kiss on his cheek. "Then that is what I will do. Buy all of th—"

"*Kiiiiiii!*" Jessie's scream was deafening in the close con-

182

fines of the bridge. Ki jerked up straight and saw the giant form filling the passage to his left. In a single, agonizing part of a second he saw the scorched flesh of Maksutova's body, the crazed eyes in the hideously blackened face, the dark fingers trembling around a revolver aimed straight at Ki's head. He saw the blur of motion at his feet, saw the blanket fall from naked shoulders, and heard the harsh cry of anger in Natalia's throat as she launched herself straight at Maksutova.

"No, Natalia—no!"

Ki's cry was lost in the shattering roar of the pistol. The slender form twisted at the waist and fell limply to the deck. Maksutova stared. A terrible sound began in his throat. In a single motion, Ki's arm jerked past his shoulder, tore the harpoon off the wall, and hurled it with every ounce of strength in his body.

The steel head struck the giant below his navel, pinned him to the wall, and buried its length clear to the wooden shaft. Maksutova howled. His body shuddered in the awful throes of pain. The pistol fell from his hand. He kicked at the floor and gripped the wooden shaft in his fists, fighting to tear it free. The more he struggled, the deeper the steel tore at his vitals.

Ki kneeled and lifted Natalia gently in his arms. He stared in disbelief at the lovely figure. Only a small, single blue smudge below her breast marred her beauty. Such a very small mark. He would kiss the hurt, bring her back, and make her laugh.

A harsh, ragged cry stuck in his throat. He reached down and wrapped her in the blanket and cradled her against his chest. Tears scalded his cheeks and blurred his vision. He cleared his eyes and looked at the giant, watched the pain tear through his body. He saw Hunter move, bend, and pick up the pistol. Hunter's face was pale as ash. He raised the weapon in a trembling hand and aimed it at Maksutova's head.

"Noooo!" Ki's voice thundered with an anger that halted Hunter in his tracks. "You . . . will . . . not . . . kill him," Ki said hoarsely. "Do you understand me? No one . . . will . . . kill him!"

"Get away from him," Jessie said calmly. "Leave him alone, Mark." She looked at Ki and saw the white hot rage in his eyes and knew she couldn't reach him. He was no longer Ki. He was someone else. He would be Ki again, but now he was a man she didn't know. She gripped Hunter's arm and led him quickly through the passageway and out into the cold evening air.

Ki sat on the floor. His legs were crossed and his back was straight. He held Natalia close. The giant clutched at his belly and shrieked in horror. Sweat glistened on his ruined face. The cords in his neck trembled. He glared at Ki and bellowed in Russian. His words meant nothing to Ki.

Ki's samurai training had taught him to fight, to fight with honor and kill when it was necessary to kill. He did not seek another man's suffering or pain. There was a dignity, an obligation, even in the death of an enemy.

Still, a shadow had crossed his heart. The shadow was the wing of a bird with great dark wings. When the wings beat the air, they left a chilling wind behind, colder than any wind that had swept the broad glacier outside.

Ki held Natalia in his arms and watched his enemy die. He shared, with Maksutova, a knowledge of the body and how it worked. He knew the giant could last a long time, that his great strength could keep him alive for hours. Yet, there would come a time when he would scarcely feel the pain, when his body would grow numb with approaching death. When that time came, Ki told himself he would control the rage and sorrow that now consumed him. He would take the path of honor, the path of the samurai warrior.

A dark and terrible thing had touched his mind, a thought from the bird with chilling wings. It told him how he could use the flickering torch Hunter had left behind to keep Maksutova screaming forever. It was an unworthy thought. And it would not bring Natalia back.

Watch for

LONE STAR AND THE WHITE RIVER CURSE

forty-first novel in the exciting
LONE STAR series from Jove

coming in January!

54